Death by Jelly Beans

by

Susie Black

The Holly Swimsuit Mystery Series

Cover Art by *The Wild Rose Press, Inc.*

The Wild Rose Press, Inc.
PO Box 708
Adams Basin, NY 14410-0708
Visit us at www.thewildrosepress.com

Publishing History
First Edition, 2024
Trade Paperback ISBN 978-1-5092-5637-2
Digital ISBN 978-1-5092-5638-9

The Holly Swimsuit Mystery Series
Published in the United States of America

Dedication

Death by Jelly Beans is dedicated to the late, great Sue Ann Kratzer and the bigger-than-life Bonnie Wilks, the two amazing colleagues who I shared all my ladies' swimwear adventures and misadventures with.
I can think of no more appropriate way to show my gratitude than to enshrine you two in my stories.
Sue Ann, I bet you'd find the pushy, sharp-tongued Sue Ellen Magee character-the buyer the swimwear industry loved to hate- who is based on you, deliciously mean but hilarious.
Bonnie, we may have called you the Empress, but I gave you a big promotion when I named you Queenie Levine and appointed you as Holly Schlivnik's venerable sidekick.
You two never let me get away with anything, and for that I am eternally grateful. You were and always will be the true embodiment of the Yentas.

Chapter One

The flagship location of Bainbridge Department Stores on Broadway between Sixth and Seventh Streets in downtown Los Angeles had not opened for business yet when I arrived. I stopped at the security desk next to the loading dock door at the back of the store and presented my photo identification to the guard. He examined the contents of my messenger bag, handed me a visitor's badge, and waved me inside through the employee entrance.

To get to my meeting with Sue Ellen Magee, the powerful, nasty my time is valuable and yours isn't Bainbridge ladies' swimwear buyer, I had to go through her department to reach the executive level elevators. I got to the entrance of the swimwear department and stopped in my tracks. I turned a one-eighty around the floor and my jaw dropped. The large department occupying the corner adjacent to the south entrance on the main floor had been transformed into an Easter wonderland.

A horseshoe-shaped open archway of countless multi-colored balloons and streamers led into the department. A series of giant-sized, pastel-colored rubber jelly beans served as stepping stones from the main aisle into the swimwear department. The stepping stones steered customers to groups of mannequins dressed in the latest swimsuits and beach cover-ups.

The mannequins stood in front of four-way displays of the same products worn by the models at strategic places on the department floor. Each mannequin nestled a plush toy Easter Bunny in the crook of one arm and an Easter basket filled with jelly beans dangled on the fingertips of the other hand.

Posters featuring various scenes of historic Catalina Island, located twenty-six miles across the ocean from Los Angeles harbor and once owned by the Wrigley family of chewing gum fame, hung suspended from the ceiling above the mannequins.

From the mannequins, the customer followed the jelly bean path to the focal point of the Easter event: A garland and flower-decorated throne where the Easter Bunny presided. Surrounded by ten packed four-way racks of swimwear and beach accessories, the throne sat in the center of the department. A wooden white picket fence with an overlay mural of pastel flowers, Easter eggs, and Easter Bunnies painted on it segregated the throne from the swimwear products. A photographer's tripod camera and spotlights stood directly in front of the throne.

A glass library table with an enormous ginger jar filled with Teenie Weenie Jelly Beanie brand jelly beans was set beside the throne. A wicker basket next to the jar held Bainbridge logo pens and contest entrance forms for customers to complete with guesses of the exact number of jelly beans in the jar. A wire cage hopper filled with completed contest entrance forms rested on the other side of the jar. Whoever guessed the exact number of jelly beans in the jar would win a thousand-dollar swimwear and beach accessory wardrobe and an all-expense paid weekend for two on Catalina Island.

On the other side of the throne, another glass library table housed an array of miniature Easter baskets filled with small packets of jelly beans for the Easter Bunny to give to children while they sat on the rabbit's lap.

Before going any further, let me introduce myself and explain my role in this tale. I am Holly Schlivnik, President of Mermaid Swimwear. We are a major supplier to Bainbridge Department Stores, and our corporate headquarters and warehouse are also located in downtown Los Angeles in the heart of the garment district.

I tool around town in a sixty-five bubblegum pink vintage convertible and live on a houseboat in Marina del Rey with my standard black poodle/canine psychiatrist Sigmund Freud. Hey, don't knock it. Siggie is an attentive listener, doesn't tell me my time is up right as I'm getting to the root of the problem, and doesn't charge a hundred and fifty bucks a session.

I checked the time and my heart pounded hard as a jackhammer. Caramba. I'd lollygagged tourist-style in Sue Ellen's department for far too long. I only had five minutes to get my tush upstairs for the meeting. I'd better hustle my bustle if I didn't want to be late. There'd be hell to pay if I dared be a minute tardy with this pain in the patootie buyer. I high-stepped it double-time to the executive-level elevator.

Apparel buyers are notorious for keeping vendors waiting. My luck, I get the one who is *never* late. Unless you're lying dead in a ditch, you better not keep this stickler for promptness waiting a minute or you're toast. Offering a valid excuse for being late still fell on deaf ears. Standing on your head and begging pathetic as a penniless pauper if only five minutes late still cut you no slack. You'd be instructed to reschedule the appointment and shown the door.

I jabbed the up button a half-dozen times, but the old-fashioned open cage-style elevator had a mind of its own. The beautiful brass inlaid doors of the slow-moving senior citizen cab in service for almost a century finally creaked open and I stepped inside. And of course, the cantankerous old elevator took its sweet time crawling to the top floor. I re-checked my watch. Merde. Only two minutes left to get to Sue Ellen's office.

Seconds before I split my spleen in anticipation of Sue Ellen's wrath, at last, the car lurched to a shaky stop. The grilled doors ground halfway open as I squeezed my derriere out of the car. I sprinted down the hall to naturally, the buyer's cube farthest on the floor from the elevator.

I careened around the corner and barreled into Sue Ellen's outer office as the clock struck nine. I screeched to a halt only to see her assistant's and clerical desks both vacant and the buyer's office door closed.

Crap on a cracker. Did I screw up the time of the meeting? If I did, Sue Ellen would skin me alive. The thought alone sent an involuntary shudder down the length of my spine. I wiped my sweaty palms on my chinos. Good grief. This meeting had disaster written all over it before it began. I needed this aggravation like I needed a bigger ass. I yanked the day planner out of my messenger bag. My heart resumed beating normally as I confirmed I had the correct appointment date and time.

Sue Ellen insisted she and her staff start work promptly at eight a.m. So, where in the Sam Hill were they? Maybe they all got called into a last-minute management meeting? No notice taped on the door, but hey, who says they'd give any thought to the value of a vendor's time? Should I wait for who knows how long or write a note and boogie? I raked my fingers through my hair. I found neither option appealing. I dawdled with indecision. What to do, what to do?

What do they say? Ask and ye shall receive? Before I came to the invariably wrong decision, the answer to the question arrived up front and personal. The door to Sue Ellen's office flew open and a six-foot tall rabbit I'd later learn named Pedro Conejo, President of Rent-A-Rabbit Characters, stalked out and bowled me over as I tried vainly to get out of his way.

The messenger bag containing samples and the presentation information fell off my shoulder and bounced across the room. I groaned as the flap of the unzipped messenger bag flipped open, scattering samples and documents and everything else inside it from one end of the room to the other.

The rabbit gripped the two ears atop the head with his paws. He yanked the headpiece straight up, ripped it off with a furious jerk, and shoved it under his right armpit. He turned, faced Sue Ellen's open door, and screamed loud enough for anyone at the mart three blocks away to hear. *"You can't prove a damned thing. Think you'll get away with this? We have a contract. I'll get you fired for this, you bitch!"*

Then the rabbit removed the left paw of his costume with his teeth and gave Sue Ellen the middle finger salute. He hurdled over my prone body splayed out on the floor and stomped out of the office without so much as an apology for knocking me over, let alone an offer to help me up.

I sat up and poked my extremities to make sure

nothing more than my pride had been injured. Satisfied my body, if not my self-respect, remained in one piece, I shook myself to get out the kinks the way Siggie does after a bath. I stretched as far as possible and grabbed the messenger bag. I spent the next five minutes crawling on all fours around the room, stuffing everything back inside the case. Note to self: Next time, zip the damned bag closed.

As I shoved the last sample back in the messenger bag, Sue Ellen's assistant came out of the buyer's office and observed me sprawled across the floor. I bit the inside of my cheek not to laugh as Abby deadpanned. "Sue Ellen will see you now."

This was gonna be one heck of a meeting. A helluva way to start a day if you were stupid enough to only have one cup of coffee before meeting with Sue Ellen Magee.

Chapter Two

The Yentas, Joan Binder, Hope Greenberg, Queenie Levine, Sonia Wilson, and I have been meeting each workday morning for coffee at A Jolt of Java in the California Apparel Mart lobby for over two years. The now-daily event started as a once-in-a-while get-together and morphed into the glue binding our group of colleagues together.

I distributed the steaming hot beverages and surveyed the Yenta table. I held my coffee cup out in front and laughed. "Drink up, ladies. I've got a story for you, and trust me, you're gonna need every drop of java."

The Yentas looked at me expectantly, yet complied. After everyone had been sufficiently fortified by a glug of caffeine, I recounted my harrowing tale. I finished and the usually non-stop yakkers sat slack-jawed into a rare silence.

As expected, quick-witted Joan was the first to re-discover her vocal cords. "Lemme get this straight. You get to Sue Ellen's for a meeting and her door is closed, and neither of her staff are in the outer office. You check the calendar and you've got the correct meeting date and time. You're deciding whether to wait or boogie and…" Joan looked over the rims of her eyeglasses for confirmation. I nodded and she continued. "And a *six-*

foot tall rabbit runs out of Sue Ellen's office and plows into you. The rabbit yanks off his headpiece, yells he's gonna get Sue Ellen fired, gives her the middle finger salute, and runs out the door while you're still sprawled across the floor."

I lifted a shoulder. "Yep. Sounds pretty crazy, huh? Believe me, you can't make this stuff up. It is exactly what happened."

Reality-driven just-the-facts-please Sonia widened her dubious eyes. "And afterward, your meeting went ahead as if *nothing* happened?"

I shook my head. "Not exactly. Normally, the Sue Ellen we all love to hate never offers any explanations, let alone apologies, for *anything*, no matter how egregious the situation." I grinned. "But yesterday for some inexplicable reason, the Queen of Mean found it necessary to explain the identity of a six-foot rabbit and why he flipped her off." I glanced around the table. "Any of you speak Spanish?"

Hope, Joan, and Sonia raised their hands.

Queenie narrowed her eyes. "I took German in high school, but what does speaking Spanish have anything to do with the rabbit?"

I bit my lip not to laugh. "Well, I found out the guy in the rabbit costume's name is Pedro Conejo. He's the President of Rent-A-Rabbit Characters." I turned to the three Spanish speakers and made a take-it-away motion with my hands. "Anyone care to translate the fellow's name from Spanish into English?"

Joan burst out laughing and slapped the table so hard half of her coffee sloshed out of the cup. "You've gotta be kidding!"

I entwined my baby fingers and held them up.

"Nope. Pinky swear. I'm not." I pointed to Queenie. "Go ahead, Joanie. Tell her."

Joan turned to Queenie and played a ta-da with her hands. "The guy's name is Peter Rabbit!"

My partner in crime at Mermaid Swimwear rolled her eyes and tsked. "Oh, come on. For crying out loud. It *must* be a stage name."

I shook my head. "Nope. I said the same thing to Sue Ellen. She pinky swore it is the guy's *legal* name."

Ditzy Swimwear showroom manager Hope pursed her lips into a funnel. "Good grief. Just imagine going through life with *such a name*. He must have been teased mercilessly in school."

Sonia shook her head. "What kind of parents stick a kid with such a laughable name?"

Joan smirked. "Ones who didn't want any children." She made air quotation marks with her fingers. "Maybe Pedro is *un accidente*?"

Perpetually optimistic Hope smiled sweetly. "If life gives you lemons, make lemonade."

"So, he and Sue Ellen got into it hot and heavy?" Queenie batted her eyes. "Gee, I'm utterly gobsmacked."

I held up an index finger. "Sue Ellen said several complaints came from parents alleging when they put their kid in the rabbit's lap, they smelled alcohol on his breath."

Sonia patted her cheeks. "Wow. Word gets out Bainbridge has a drunk Easter Bunny working with kids, it's gonna kill their promo."

Hope asked, "So, Sue Ellen fired him?"

I shook my head. "Not yet. All she has are some complaints, but no proof. He didn't stagger his way through the department to the throne, fall on his face, drop a kid, or slur his words. So, all she's done is threaten to fire him if they get more complaints. For now, at least, he's still on the job. It turns out that this is a good-sized company and employs a lot of people. He doesn't normally work the gigs himself anymore, but he's got a handful of employees out with the flu and he stepped in to help pick up the slack. His company is locked into a long-term, all-store contract with Bainbridge. This is the first time the store received any complaints."

Sonia widened her eyes. "It might be only the first time the store had complaints, but they can't afford that kind of bad publicity." Sonia poked a finger into her cleavage. "If I brought *my kids* to see the Easter Bunny at their store and I smelled booze on the bunny's breath, let me assure you, I'd never step foot in a Bainbridge Department Store again." She jutted her chin. "And, I'd be sure to tell all my friends with kids to do the same."

I held up two fingers. "Sue Ellen said the guy has been warned twice. The next time, contract or no contract, he and his rabbits will be gone."

Hope blew the air out of her cheeks. "Yeah, but to break a contract and not get sued, she'll still need proof."

Sonia narrowed her eyes. "If he comes to work already drunk, and doesn't do anything stupid, it'll be tough. A regular he said/she said is hard to prove. But if he's dumb enough to sneak a drink while on the job, he's toast. Security cameras are everywhere in the store and they will nail him. And as to breaking a contract? Not as difficult as you'd think. These days, most contracts contain a morals clause. If Sue Ellen proves the rabbit to be drunk on the job, all Pedro Conejo can use the pages of his contract for will be to line the floor of his rabbit hutch."

Queenie tapped an index finger to the tip of her nose. "And if it comes to that, how does Bainbridge replace forty Easter Bunnies at the drop of a hat?"

Joan put her hands over the top of her head and wiggled her fingers. "I bet Sue Ellen *convinces* all her vendors *to hop* in to save the day."

Queenie made a sour face. "Cows will sprout wings before you'd get me into one of those getups."

I surveyed the table. "You guys been on Sue Ellen's floor lately? I went through the department on my way to the meeting. The Easter extravaganza display turned out gorgeous. She used foam rubber jelly beans as stepping stones for customers to meander through the department on a path ending at the Easter Bunny throne. And next to the throne is an enormous ginger jar full of jelly beans. Customers fill out a form to guess the number of jelly beans in the jar and the one who guesses the exact amount wins a swimwear wardrobe worth a thousand dollars and an all-expenses paid weekend for two to Catalina Island."

Joan sighed. "No wonder all the vendors coughed up *so much* co-op money for advertising."

Hope shrugged. "A jelly bean theme for a promotion? Not a big surprise. It's a well-known fact Sue Ellen is bonkers for jelly beans."

I nodded. "A gigantic jar filled with Teenie Weenie Jelly Beenie Jelly Beans is always on her desk. I never gave it a second thought. Lots of people keep a jar of candy on their desks, including me." I glanced around the table. "Yesterday her office looked as though a jelly bean candy store exploded. She has a jelly bean paperweight and memo pads in the shape of a jelly bean on her desk. Posters, photos, and paintings of jelly beans decorate her office walls. She has a couple of coffee table books with photos and a history of the jelly bean on the conference table. A collection of every kind of canister and dispenser imaginable loaded with jelly beans is on the credenza. A few of the dispensers are antiques."

Sonia said, "I always worked with Sue Ellen in the mart. Until I went to her office, who knew Sue Ellen was such a jelly bean fiend?"

I gave the group the big eyes. "Boy, is she ever. Sue Ellen said Teenie Weenie Jelly Beenie Jelly Beans have been her favorite candy since childhood. She contacted the company and told them she'd been a lifelong fan. "With her demanding personality, Sue Ellen can be…" I grinned and wiggled my fingers into quotation marks in the air. "Let's be kind and call it *convincing* if she wants something. I bet she wore the company president down in no time flat, and it didn't take too much arm twisting to get him to provide all the jelly beans for all the stores for the event on the come and sponsor the Easter Extravaganza along with all us swimwear suppliers." I fanned my hands. "It certainly explains her request for us to design a capsule collection of junior swimsuits in a jelly bean print. The reason for my appointment yesterday was to show her the production samples."

I swiped a wrist across my forehead. "Thank goodness the styles turned out adorable. We put on an extra line of sewers to ensure on-time delivery. We're shipping the all-store order today. The goods will be on the floor for the whole month. The capsule collection is going to be the grand finale of the fashion shows at all forty stores on the last day of the event."

Sonia flapped her arms in the air like a bird. "Boy, those styles better *fly* out of the stores. One month is not a lot of sell-through time."

I held out my hands in supplication. "No kidding. It's risky. I said the same thing to Sue Ellen but she refused to take no for an answer."

Joan puckered her lips as though she bit into a grapefruit section. "Too bad having such a sweet tooth for jelly beans didn't sweeten Sue Ellen's sour personality."

I nodded as bouncy as a bobblehead doll. "You're not whistling Dixie. Miss Warm and Fuzzy never asked if I had been hurt, let alone apologize for the guy's outrageous behavior." I smiled tightly. "Her only concern? Whether I planned to sue either the rabbit or the store."

Chapter Three

Two Days Later:

Between bites of a gooey Philly Cheesesteak sandwich consumed at a six-table greasy-spoon dive located on a narrow side street a few blocks from the mart, I gave Queenie the lowdown on a call from Sue Ellen's assistant earlier in the morning. "Sue Ellen is absolutely over the moon with our selling. After being on the floor for only two days, the jelly bean Easter promotional group sold through at thirty percent. Two styles in the group beat the department sell-through average by six points. Abby asked if we could deliver another twenty-four hundred units between the two best retailing styles in a week."

Queenie's eyes bugged. "Holy cow! Talk about some incredible selling! Do we have any fabric left? Can we turn twenty-four hundred units this fast?"

I shrugged. "I dunno. I'll ask production. Even if the piece goods are in stock and we can produce that many units in such a short time, I'm not sure I want to take the order."

Queenie's voice went up a dozen octaves. "*Why the heck not*? We *are* in business to *sell* swimsuits to stores. *Remember?*"

I swallowed my impatience and plastered an indulgent smile on my lips. "Yes, Miss Smarty Pants. Far be it from me to turn away business, but you've gotta admit that's *a lot of jelly beans*. Unless they sold out during the Easter season, I don't see that time-sensitive kind of style holding its own after the holiday is over. And if the sales drop off and Sue Ellen marks the reorder units down, rest assured she'll develop amnesia as to who *insisted* on bringing more in, as well as have her hand out for markdown money."

Queenie grinned. "Who ya gonna hire to tell the bikini bitch she's making a mistake buying more?"

No kidding. Even with the store's best interest in mind, only an idiot questioned Sue Ellen's forecasting ability. My dad always said, if in doubt, punt. So, in true Schlivnik fashion, I tap-danced my way out of an answer by telling the truth: I'd get back to her.

Instead of returning to the mart after lunch, I pointed in the direction of Bainbridge Department Store. "Let's take a detour and go through the swimwear department. You can see the jelly bean group on the floor and give me your fifty cents worth of advice on this re-order. Maybe my gut is wrong this time."

We entered the store on the south side where the swimwear department is housed. I stopped short at the Easter arch entrance to Sue Ellen's department. My eyes bugged watching Ditzy Swimwear owner Michael Chennault undressing one of the mannequins. He stripped *our hottest-selling jelly bean promotional suit* off the mannequin and re-dressed the dummy with one of Ditzy's styles. While he changed the mannequin, his designer took photos of every vendor's display. After he changed the mannequin, Michael moved all of the Ditzy Swimwear four-way racks from the back of the department to the front, adjacent to the mannequin, and moved all of our racks back to where his styles had been.

Fists clenched, I stalked into the arch, ready for bear.

Queenie clamped her fingers around my left bicep and dug her talon-sharp nails into my skin. "Down, girl."

I squealed like a stuck pig. "*Have you lost your mind?*" I pointed a j'accuse right index finger at the two perpetrators. "Look what they're doing, for crying out loud! No wonder Louis left Michael his entire estate. The apple didn't fall far from the tree. Michael is as sneaky and unscrupulous as his lying sack of crap cheating dead brother."

Queenie tsked. "Now, now. Isn't it you who always lectures me one shouldn't speak badly of the dead?"

"Every rule has exceptions."

I'd never work for a slug like Michael Chennault. His reputation is as bad as his late brother's. It is the reason I left Ditzy after Rob Bachmann sold Michael the company. I shivered. "The slimy guy gives me the creeps. It's beyond me why Hope and Buster stayed."

Queenie elbowed me in the ribs and motioned to the Easter Bunny entering the swimwear department and heading straight for the jar of jelly beans. The bunny surreptitiously looked around and took a small flask out of a pouch in his costume. He brought the flask to the mouth opening of the costume and glugged a healthy slug. He shoved the flask back in the pouch and wiped his whiskers with the back of his paw. He sauntered over to the jar filled with jelly beans. He removed the lid, scooped out two pawfuls of jelly beans, and shoved them into the mouth opening of the costume.

The bunny turned to sit on the throne and watched Michael re-dressing the mannequin with his Ditzy style, then drop our suit on the ground and kick it behind the dummy. Pedro got off the throne and confronted Michael. The two traded words and got into a shoving match. Always in great shape, gym rat Michael stood a good three inches taller than the-going-to-seed bunny and outweighed him by at least thirty pounds.

I yanked my arm to get out of Queenie's clutches and growled deep in my throat. "Let go of me. I'm gonna kill the jerk."

I wriggled like a worm on a hook, but Queenie held onto my arm with a vise-hold grip. She clucked her tongue "You'll do no such thing. First of all, Michael is twice your size. The big goon could break you in half with one hand." She grinned evilly. "If you want to ensure his demise, let Sue Ellen do it for you."

I pointed to Michael as he stepped over prone Pedro writhing on the floor and kicked the bunny in the tail for good measure. Then Mr. Slimeball Chennault and the woman strolled carefree through the swimwear department and exited out the other end of the store. I snarled. "Fanfreakingtastic. Since *you* let them escape, Michael gets away with it."

Queenie grinned and pointed to the bank of security cameras mounted around the ceiling all aimed into the swimwear department. She checked the time. "Let your fingers do your talking. Take out your cell and call Sue Ellen. Say you're on her floor and are reporting a major security breach. Tell her to have the head of security send her the film from the cameras in her department for the last three hours. That ought to cover the time Michael and his cohort monkeyed around with Sue Ellen's stock. I'm sure she'll find the footage quite entertaining."

I pointed to Pedro stumbling and bumbling around as he attempted to hoist himself off the floor. "The film will also catch Pedro in the act of nipping the sauce. This ought to cook the rabbit's goose." I put my hands behind my head and wiggled my fingers. "Joan is right. Don't be surprised if we get a call to help out as replacement Easter Bunnies if Pedro and company get the boot."

Queenie shook her head. "Not necessarily. The film doesn't identify the *beverage* he drank out of the flask. And if it was booze, he ate two handfuls of jelly beans to mask the liquor smell. He denies drinking on the job and Sue Ellen is unable to prove otherwise. The security film might actually help Pedro keep his job."

I narrowed my eyes. "You nipping the sauce yourself?"

She turned up her nose. "Hardly. I enjoy a good scotch on the rocks with a twist as much as the next gal, but I *never* imbibe before cocktail hour. Why?"

I rolled my eyes. "It is the only explanation for such a stupid comment."

Queenie sniffed. "Not at all. Michael probably saved Pedro's ass. The bunny can easily turn this around in his favor by saying he's a hero and tried to stop Michael from vandalizing the department."

I rubbed my chin. "It never crossed my mind, but you're right. Michael might end up the big loser, not Pedro. Pedro's biggest offense is helping himself to a couple of pawfuls of jelly beans. Nobody with a brain would mess with Sue Ellen's department. I bet she threatens to throw Ditzy out of the store." I grimaced. "Word circulates in the market and starts an avalanche of cancellations. The domino effect puts him out of business in the blink of an eye."

Queenie clucked her tongue. "Don't lose any sleep worrying over Michael. You don't have to hold a benefit for him. His brother left him a fortune."

I nodded my agreement. "No kidding. As the sole heir to his brother's estate, Michael inherited a bucket of bucks, all the properties, and Louis's fleet of race cars. Michael served as head of Louis's pit crew. I'll ask Hope if Michael races the cars now or if he sold them." I tapped my lip. "Maybe Michael kept the cars, only he stayed in the pit crew and hired a professional race driver?"

Queenie rubbed her hands together. "He inherited a big bundle of bucks. Hope said Michael bought Ditzy *for cash*. Any idea what he did before he bought Ditzy?"

I nodded. "A partner in A-to-Z garment delivery, a local delivery service he owned with his wife's brother. The industry rumor is he and his brother-in-law are tied to the mafia. At one time, they controlled virtually all the local apparel deliveries."

Queenie widened her eyes. "So, if he still owns part of it, he threatens to withhold or delay deliveries to stores who don't give him enough business." She pointed to Sue Ellen's floor. "I bet it's his end game. He's not just planning to knock off his competitors. He's planning to steal their floor space by threatening Sue Ellen's deliveries."

I slapped my cheeks. "Crap on a cracker. You may be right. And don't be surprised if he goes after *us first*. Michael still got a burr up his butt that I left Ditzy to work at Mermaid after he bought the company."

Queenie clucked her tongue. "Let's not get ahead of ourselves." Queenie tapped her index finger on the tip of her nose. "Your nana always said don't look for trouble. It will find you all on its own. Right?"

My heart warmed at the memory. "Yep. A true Nana classic."

Queenie played a ta-da with her hands. "Straight from the lips of the wise one."

I smiled. "The wisest."

I blanched. "I don't give a flying fig about Michael Chennault, but I'd hate to see Hope and Buster and all the other employees hurt if Ditzy went out of business."

Queenie shrugged. "It might be a blessing in disguise for their careers not being associated with scummy Michael. They're all seasoned professionals with good reputations. They'll easily land with another supplier."

"You're right."

I pulled the cell phone out of my purse and made the call.

Chapter Four

I served the Yentas their cuppas and took my seat across from Hope. "You'll never guess who I ran into today on my morning walk with Sigmund."

The Yentas universally shrugged their ignorance.

I said, "Abby Blane."

Joan gawked. "As in *Sue Ellen's assistant* Abby?"

I nodded. "Yep. One and the same."

Queenie cocked her head. "Does she live in Marina del Rey? If she does, it's odd I've never seen her around. I've lived in the marina for ten years. It's a small area. You'd think I'd have run into her at the supermarket or drug store at least once." Queenie pointed a spoon at me. I shook my head after she asked, "Before today, did you?"

Sonia pursed her lips. "The marina is a pricey neighborhood. Unless she comes from money or has a houseful of roommates, how does she afford to live at the beach on a buyer's assistant salary?"

Joan drummed the table rat-a-tat-tat with a spoon and mused. "No way."

Queenie tapped her finger on the tip of her nose. "Then why in the world is she at the marina before the crack of dawn?"

I bent my elbows horizontally and moved my arms in and out. "She's a rower. She rents a scull from the

UCLA boathouse at the end of the main channel. She rows every morning for an hour before going to work."

Hope held her arms out and flexed her biceps boxer-style. "Ah, a rower. No wonder Abby is strong as an ox. We are in the same art class on Tuesday evenings at The Women's Village on Broadway, next to the Endicott Fashion Modeling School. The art class teaches modern sculpture using junk, common household items, and tools as the artwork components. She lifted a heavy length of pipe as easily as if it was a sheet of paper."

Sonia said, "Abby set an assembly line on her desk to fill those little souvenir baskets with cellophane-wrapped jelly beans for the table next to the Easter Bunny to give to the kids. And filled Sue Ellen's desktop canister with jelly beans. Sonia grinned. "Abby said our Miss Congeniality gets especially crabby if, Heaven forbids, it isn't always full."

Joan wrinkled her nose. "*Abby* filled the baskets and not the mousy-faced clerk?" Joan puckered her lips. "Preparing Easter baskets is a menial job better suited for a clerk than a buyer's assistant."

Sonia nodded. "I said the same thing. Abby said she didn't care for the way the clerk fixed them the first time. She said she ended up redoing them all, so she'd rather just do them herself the next time."

Joan glanced at me. "You and Siggie walk the opposite side of the marina from the UCLA boathouse on your way to the Washington Pier. Did she row down your basin?"

I shook my head. "Uh-uh. She stood in line behind me at A Jolt of Java across from the Washington Street pier. We chatted for a few minutes after we got our coffees."

Hope asked, "Why go clear over to the other side of the marina for coffee? There must be a coffee shop nearer to the boathouse."

I nodded. "Absolutely. Only she prefers A Jolt of Java to the coffee shop near the boathouse and it's the only Jolt location in the marina." I wrinkled my forehead. "Boy, she is one frustrated little camper."

Hope scrunched her nose. "Frustrated about only one A Jolt of Java in the marina? Maybe she shouldn't be so picky." Hope waved her arm around the coffee store. "I prefer A Jolt of Java as much as the next gal, but there's something to be said for convenience. After all, it's *only coffee*, for goodness' sake. It's not a fine wine."

I rolled my eyes. "Good grief. Not the *coffee*. Her *job*."

Joan snorted. "What *normal* person *wouldn't be frustrated* working for the Queen of Mean? There isn't enough money minted for *me* to work for Sue Ellen Magee."

Queenie wrinkled her nose. "No one's holding a gun to Abby's head. If it's so awful, why doesn't she quit?"

I panned the table. "She has invested almost two years in the executive training program. If she quits, she'd be forced to start from scratch doing something else. And she's lost valuable time impossible to make up to establish herself in a career."

Sonia asked, "What did she do before working for Sue Ellen?"

I said, "She earned an MBA from UCLA with an emphasis on corporate management. She entered the Bainbridge executive training program right out of graduate school. Sue Ellen got assigned as her supervisor." I widened my eyes. "Believe it or not, she *loves* working for Sue Ellen." The Yentas' jaws dropped. "She said Sue Ellen knows her stuff and is an excellent teacher. Abby says while Sue Ellen is often abrupt, and patience isn't one of her strong suits, she's not abusive. She's learned a lot from her, and isn't interested in changing supervisors."

Hope frowned. "So, then what's her beef?"

"She says she has met every milestone on time and fulfilled every program requirement for promotion. She's the first one in and the last one to leave every day. She never complains about any of the grunt work and gets every assignment done, no matter how menial, on time, as instructed, and has gone above and beyond the program requirements trying to impress Sue Ellen. Yet Sue Ellen has passed over her twice and promoted two less qualified assistants in the same program for less time. According to Abby, they got promoted instead of her because they kissed Sue Ellen's ass."

Joan played a ta-da with her hands. "Well, then all she has to do is pucker up!"

I shook my head. "She wants to earn the promotion, not suck up her way to it."

Joan muttered, "A self-righteous moron. If she wants the promotion bad enough, the end justifies the means."

Sonia asked, "Has she talked to Sue Ellen about it? Maybe Sue Ellen has a good reason."

I nodded. "Abby says Sue Ellen acknowledges her accomplishments but says that she is not ready for promotion. Sue Ellen says she has to put in the sweat time."

Joan rubbed her chin. "Or maybe she's too good at the job, and Sue Ellen doesn't want to lose her and have to train someone else," Joan smirked. "Don't put it past Cruella de Ville to keep Abby as an indentured servant for as long as possible."

Chapter Five

I met with Ike Loach, our head of production, regarding Sue Ellen's reorder request. The good news for the world's most difficult-to-please buyer? We have enough fabric to fill all those units and turn the goods in a week. The bad news: We can do it only if she'd agree to take all the units in the one style with the yield taking less yardage. Or, if she insisted on twenty-four hundred units divided between the two styles, she must accept a design change from all-over pattern bodies to printed bras and solid briefs for both styles. Production sewed samples with the printed bras and solid briefs to show Sue Ellen. This ought to be a fun conversation. Not.

Remarkably, Sue Ellen made no demand for us to find a way to ship her goods the original way. Must be a catch. *Conciliatory* is *not* a word found in the Queen of Mean's vocabulary.

I walked through the Easter arch into the swimwear department and spied Sue Ellen, Abby, and four men hovering over a large schematic diagram spread out on one of the glass library tables. Sue Ellen instructed the merchandise floor setters to return the department to the way it had been set up before Michael Chennault and his cohort converted it into a Ditzy Swimwear store.

Sue Ellen pointed to my messenger bag. "I presume those are the samples for my approval?" I nodded and she tapped the diagram with a pencil. "We're almost finished. Go on up to my office and get the presentation ready. The door is closed but unlocked. We'll be up in five minutes."

I gave her the okay sign and headed for the executive elevator. I got to Sue Ellen's office and stopped short of the doorjamb. The door was wide open. I leaned in and my eyes bugged as *Michael Chennault* pulled a stack of files out of the file cabinet behind Sue Ellen's desk. I stepped back out and angled my body so I could see him, but he couldn't see me.

Michael closed the cabinet drawer and stacked the files on Sue Ellen's desk. He separated one file and pushed the others to the side. He sat down, opened the file, and helped himself to a handful of Sue Ellen's jelly beans from the candy jar sitting on the desk. He went through each file and photographed the contents with his phone app.

Sue Ellen and Abby arrived just as Michael finished photographing the third file. Sue Ellen tried an unsuccessful end around after I put my arm out school crossing guard-style to stop them from going inside. Her face turned eggplant purple as I made a shushing motion with my finger and pointed to Michael making himself right at home at her desk.

Sue Ellen whispered to Abby. "Go next door and call security. Tell them it's an emergency."

Two minutes later, Sue Ellen turned to me and squared her shoulders. "I can't wait for security. It might take an hour for them to get around to answering our call. This is my office. And my problem. I'm going in and confront him." She clenched and unclenched her fists. "You stay here where he can't see you and be my witness."

I grinned. "You really want a witness to you murdering him with your bare hands?"

Sue Ellen winked wickedly. "Hell yeah. This is gonna be fun."

Sue Ellen stalked into her office unannounced. Michael Chennault turned sheet white when the Bitch of Bikinis smacked the corner of her desk and sneered. "Looking for something in particular or are you just naturally nosy?"

Fast on his feet, Michael quickly regained his composure. He held up the Ditzy Swimwear folder and waved it under Sue Ellen's nose. "Yeah, I'm looking for something particular. My revised order with the increased units we discussed with *our new arrangement.*" Michael pulled a fat envelope out of his sports jacket interior pocket with the initials SEM scrawled across the front and thrust it at Sue Ellen.

Sue Ellen Magee is a lot of things. Abrupt, nasty, and demanding. But the Queen of Mean is as straight a shooter as it gets. Every supplier *earned* their place on her floor. Her business isn't for sale, and neither is she.

She leaned in for a closer look at him. "Are you on drugs or something?"

He snarled, "What the hell are you talking about?"

She pointed to the envelope and shrugged. "Must be the only explanation."

He waved the envelope under her nose again. "Don't play dumb. A deal is a deal." Michael glared. "And you're gonna keep your end of it or else...you know the consequences."

Sue Ellen rolled her eyes. "In your dreams. Our only *deal* is you stay out of my department and I don't prosecute you for trespassing and attempted theft." She clucked her tongue. "Since you violated the terms of the deal, it's now off the table. Consider your open orders canceled." She snatched the Ditzy Swimwear file out of Michael's hand and waved it like a flag. "Congratulations, Mr. Chennault. Effect immediately, you and your line are no longer on the Bainbridge Department Stores vendor matrix."

Ice water must run through the woman's veins. Sue Ellen is maybe five inches taller than me. Michael could easily snap her in half with one hand and not break into a sweat. I'd have wet myself by now.

Michael's jaw dropped. "You can't be serious. We're ready to ship six thousand units of reorder styles tomorrow. We worked overtime and focused on your order at the expense of other stores to meet your tight delivery. And now at the eleventh hour, you're cancelling the order?" Michael jutted his jaw. "When elephants fly! We're not accepting the cancelation."

Sue Ellen smiled a combination of amusement and smugness. "Knock yourself out. But understand this: The goods will be refused at the loading dock."

Michael snapped. "I'll go over your head to management. I'll go to the President of the store if need be. I'll get you fired for this."

Always quick on the uptake, Sue Ellen gave as good as she got. She rewarded Michael with a round of applause as she retorted. "Fantastic news. I hope you do go all the way to the top. The senior executives should find the security footage of your shenanigans in my department quite entertaining. After pulling that outrageous stunt, your chances of *ever* getting back into the store go from slimsky to nonesky."

All of a sudden Mr. Big Shot was reduced to whining like a toddler who didn't get his way. "What am I supposed to do with these goods now?"

Sue Ellen grinned wide as a Jack O'Lantern. "Don't tempt me."

I shoved a fist into my mouth to prevent laughing out loud. Who needs a soap opera novella on Estrella TV if you have a front-row seat to your own?

Sue Ellen shrugged. "What you do with them isn't my problem. Your failure to consider the consequences of your moronic behavior is not my concern. I'm sure you'll find another home for the goods." Sue Ellen smirked. "And if not, respectfully, shove them where the sun don't shine for all I care."

Michael glared. "I am still a partner in A-to-Z delivery. If you don't take those goods, I'll make sure Bainbridge doesn't receive another unit of apparel regardless of the category from any local manufacturer forever or until the store fires you." He smiled like a shark. "Bainbridge may be a big player, but even Bainbridge can't sell empty hangers."

Sue Ellen rolled her eyes. "Bainbridge management won't lose any sleep over your baseless threats. We're the biggest store in the city. With a caliber of buying power like ours at stake, suppliers will find another way to deliver our goods. If necessary, vendors will put the goods in their cars and deliver them to us on their own. They're in business to ship goods to their accounts, not to keep A to Z in business."

Michael cocked a brow and held up the envelope. "This isn't over. Not by a long shot. Everyone has their price, Miss High and Mighty. Including you."

Sue Ellen simpered with the confidence of a well-fed cat. "Stay out of my store, stay off my floor, stay out of my office." She wrapped a protective arm around the jar filled with jelly beans on her desk. "And keep your mitts out of my candy jar or I'll have you arrested."

Michael smacked his fist into the palm of his hand. "I'll skin the freaking rabbit alive for this."

Sue Ellen snorted as loud as a hungry hog. *"The rabbit?* You wish. Wanna blame someone for getting thrown outta my store? Look in the mirror. Security cameras filmed all your shenanigans. The rabbit's only crime? Swiping two pawfuls of jelly beans."

Just as Michael lunged at Sue Ellen, two big apes with no necks dressed in Bainbridge Department Store security uniforms strode into the buyer's office.

Sue Ellen pointed to Michael. "Trash day isn't until tomorrow, but this garbage must be disposed of immediately. Confiscate his cell phone and throw him out of the store. If he gives you any trouble, call the police and press charges for trespassing and attempted theft."

The two huge security guards, who dwarfed Michael, motioned for him to hand over his cell phone. Michael refused and the younger guard made a sudden, slick move and caught arrogant Michael unawares. The guard twisted Michael into a nifty behind-the-back armlock while the older one frisked him and yanked the cell out of the back pocket of Michael's pants. The guards sandwiched Michael between them and stiff-marched him kicking and screaming toward the door in a perp walk.

Michael rotated his upper body around and yelled, "You are toast! I'll see you're fired or I'll see you dead."

I walked into Sue Ellen's office as the security detail

clamped plastic handcuffs on Michael's wrists twisted behind his back. I came face to face with him as the guards hustled him out. Michael's dark eyes sparked with a combination of humiliation and outrage. He growled. "Take advantage of this and you'll wish you'd never been born. You've been warned."

Sue Ellen clapped with impatience. "Chop, chop, Schlivnik. It's about time you graced me with your presence." I grinned as she smacked her palm on the desk and barked. "Let's get the show on the road already. Bring out the damned samples before you miss the freaking delivery date."

Atta girl. You're on a roll. The real deal and not some cheap imitation. The Sue Ellen Magee we all love to hate.

Chapter Six

Ditzy Swimwear's expulsion from Bainbridge Department Stores was the hot topic on the eleventh floor of the mart. The wannabe vultures on the swimwear aisle wasted no time pecking at Ditzy's carcass in the hopes of replacing the outcast brand on the floor of the biggest, most powerful retailer in Los Angeles.

I distributed the Yentas' coffees and related the unbelievable series of events leading to Ditzy's demise at Bainbridge. I finished telling the tale and cast a glance of pity at Hope. Her skin tone was as gray as yesterday's oatmeal and her eyes sunk cadaver-deep in their sockets. Cutting to the chase? She looked like overcooked crap.

Hope gulped a gigantic glug of caffeinated courage and shook her head. "What the hell was that moron Michael thinking?" Hope clucked her tongue. "Michael acts more like a mafia boss than an apparel manufacturer." Hope surveyed the table. "When Michael finished ranting and raving at Buster and me, he called his lawyer." She rolled her eyes. "The idiot wanted to sue Bainbridge! Thank the Goddess the lawyer talked him down from the ledge. He has no case. He's lucky Sue Ellen chose not to press charges. Then he announced a hare-brained idea to contact Sue Ellen's management and demand she be fired. Buster and I headed him off for the moment. Then suddenly, Michael changed tactics completely."

Sonia cocked her head the same way Siggie does when he's trying to understand. "Changed tactics?"

Hope said, "Abby and I went to our art class last night. She told me Michael sent Sue Ellen a one-hundred-pound gift basket of Teenie Weenie Jelly Beenie Jelly Beans."

Sonia slapped her cheeks. "Good grief. Even for jelly bean addict Sue Ellen, it's a lifetime supply."

Joan laughed. "You've gotta give the devil his due. He came up with the perfect bribe."

Queenie wrinkled her nose. "Or knowing the Queen of Mean, more like throwing gasoline on a fire. Did straight-as-an-arrow Sue Ellen go batshit crazy?"

Hope shook her head. "She never saw it. Sue Ellen was in a meeting when the gift basket was delivered. Abby intercepted the package and hid it."

Sonia tapped the side of her head. "Smart move."

Joan snorted. "Unless Michael is expecting a thank-you card."

Hope smiled tightly. "He'll be waiting a long time for one then. Our head of shipping gave me a heads-up. Michael instructed him to ship the reorder Sue Ellen canceled. I've no idea what Michael thought he'd accomplish by shipping goods guaranteed to be refused at the Bainbridge dock. If an envelope stuffed with cash failed to change her mind and he thought a jelly bean bribe would, he's out of his mind. If Sue Ellen was pissed before, when she is notified that those canceled goods hit her dock, Michael ain't seen nuthin' yet. Every time the phone rings, I am expecting it to be Sue Ellen screaming at the top of her lungs."

Queenie and I locked eyes. Sue Ellen gave us a six-thousand-unit order late yesterday on immediate delivery, in-stock goods. No doubt it replaced the styles she canceled with Ditzy. Once Michael gets a sniff, my already tenuous relationship with him is guaranteed to go directly down the crapper.

Joan wrinkled her forehead. "Just imagine the chaos at Sue Ellen's loading dock when all those canceled goods arrive with no purchase order or distribution instructions in the system. That ought to send Miss Congeniality completely over the edge."

I gulped. "She was already professionally pissed off at Michael. This ought to make her homicidal. I pity anyone else who has the misfortune of having to deal with her now."

Joan nodded. "No kidding. I delivered model samples for the fashion show yesterday afternoon. I cut through the swimwear department and ran into Sue Ellen. Good thing no customers were nearby. She stood next to the half-empty jelly bean jar and ripped the rabbit a new one. Sue Ellen told me later that Abby goes through the swim department floor twice a day to check on the number of pens, contest forms, and little Easter baskets for the rabbit to hand out to the kids. The contest is to guess the *exact number* of jelly beans in the jar. Despite repeated warnings, the rabbit has apparently mooched half of the jelly beans out of the jar by the end of his shift. So, not only must the jar of jelly beans be replenished every night, the contest legitimacy is in question because the exact number of jelly beans in the jar keeps changing."

Sonia put her right hand at her belly button and hovered her left hand a few inches above the top of her head. "The jelly bean jar is huge. It's maybe this tall and probably eight inches around. I bet it holds at least five hundred jelly beans. Maybe more. So, if the bunny has an eight-hour shift with two breaks and a lunch hour, he's munching a helluva lot of jelly beans every day if the jar is half-empty every night."

Queenie widened her eyes. "If the booze didn't do it, he must be flying high as a kite on a sugar high. Hopefully, he's not diabetic."

Hope nodded. "You're right. Unless the Bainbridge candy department has a lot of jelly beans in stock or the jelly bean company keeps replenishing their supply, Sue Ellen might be hard-pressed to refill the jar every day." Hope shivered. "Maybe Abby will be forced to fess up about Michael's gift basket if they run short on jelly beans."

Joan grinned. "Sue Ellen running out of jelly beans? Not a chance. Abby replenishes Sue Ellen's stash *every day*. The jar on her desk is enormous. And she has all those dispensers in her office full of jelly beans too. If all else fails, she delves into her stash to replenish the contest jar. Sue Ellen told the bunny she was staying late to prepare for a meeting and would *personally* replenish the jelly beans in the jar before she left for the day, so she *knew* it would be filled to the top. She warned the rabbit if the jelly bean jar needs replenishment again, he's done, contract be damned."

Queenie asked, "And the Easter Bunny's response?"

Joan widened her eyes. "He yanked off the costume head and told her to shove her threats up her ass. He stomped away and yelled over his shoulder he was going to human resources to lodge a formal complaint of harassment and get her fired."

Queenie shook her head. "He is such a moron.

Between the parental complaints and the security tapes, the rabbit doesn't stand a chance. The store is gonna back Sue Ellen all the way."

Joan wiggled her hands over the top of her head and snuffled her nose. "Better practice your bunny rabbit imitations, girls. Sue Ellen knows the *exact number* of jelly beans it takes to fill the jar. If the jar is missing any jelly beans this morning, the Easter bunny is a dead duck."

Chapter Seven

Her Royal Highness summoned me to grace her by my presence to finalize the jelly bean bikini promotional reorder. We had a production meeting right before my appointment with her that was guaranteed to go over time. So, I called Sue Ellen back to reschedule our meeting.

Abby answered the phone and said Sue Ellen was in a meeting with her management and human resources. This must have been the meeting she said she stayed late to prepare for.

Even though Abby was alone, she whispered. "You didn't hear it from me, but Sue Ellen is in hot water over this Pedro Conejo complaint. He threatened to sue the store for harassment if they didn't fire Sue Ellen. Human Resources didn't back Sue Ellen the way she thought they would. She didn't get fired, but she received a warning. The complaint and the warning went into her employment record file. Talk about bad timing. Sue Ellen is up for a promotion and a nice bump up in pay. The word around the buying office cube is her promotion has been *indefinitely* shelved. Management told Sue Ellen she won't be getting a promotion until she improves her poor people and management skills."

Suffice it to say, the bitch of bikinis was never going to win a Miss Congeniality award. I laughed out loud. "If that's the criteria, she'll see a promotion after elephants fly. I bet Sue Ellen is fit to be tied."

Abby giggled. "Pedro is lucky he didn't show up in our office. Sue Ellen is mad enough to whack the guy. She's over at Human Resources with our divisional merchandise manager now fighting the decision."

Fanfreakingtastic. Lucky me. A meeting with an already pissed-off Sue Ellen Magee. I sighed. "Thanks for the heads up. Don't bother telling her I called to change the appointment. I'll move some things around and make it happen at the original meeting time."

****

I cut through the swimwear department on my way to the executive-level elevator and glanced at the jelly bean jar on the library table adjacent to the throne. I eyeballed the jar at one-third empty. I shook my head. Despite her Human Resources warning, as soon as Sue Ellen finds out, the Easter Bunny is toast.

I dragged my eyes over to the throne. The Easter Bunny sat slumped over with his chin resting on his chest and his body listing to the right. Good grief. A double-whammy. Not only did he dip into the jelly beans again after being warned not to, but he fell asleep on the job—no doubt in a booze-infused slumber.

Why should I give a flying fig about the jerk who bowled me over without an apology, let alone helping me up? Yet a stab of unexpected pity pierced my heart. I checked the time. I still had a few minutes before my command performance. Maybe I could rouse the poor guy and give him a chance to concoct another story Sue Ellen might buy—unless the security cameras sealed his fate.

I laid my messenger bag on the library table next to

the throne and gently shook the rabbit's left shoulder. Nothing doing. I shook him again. This time a bit harder. I put my lips next to his ears and implored him. "*Pedro, wake up.*" Zilch. Geesh, how much booze did the guy chug? Or maybe booze isn't the culprit. Perhaps the guy had a late night before or he is just one helluva sound sleeper? Oddly, he wasn't snoring, but I attributed it to his neck bent down and his head dangling over his body.

I shook him again and got nothing for my trouble. His chest wasn't rising and falling. Good gravy. Was the guy breathing? I passed my hand over the costume's mouth opening, but one so small I couldn't tell. I clasped a paw to check for a pulse, but the heavy gauge costume fabric was too thick to detect one.

I checked my watch. No more time to crap around trying to help this idiot or I'd be late for my meeting. Despite my efforts to rouse him, the guy hadn't so much as twitched. Annoyance coupled with dread tied my stomach in sailor's knots. I panned the department. No one was around except the rabbit and me.

The Goddess short-changed me in the height department but compensated by blessing me with a deep voice and a strong set of pipes. I put my lips next to his ear and shouted loud enough to wake the dead. "*Pedro! Wake up!*"

I grabbed the rabbit by the shoulder and shook him with all my might. The guy didn't move an inch. I grasped his arm tightly and yanked it hard trying to right him. Good grief. The bunny was stiff as a board. I might as well try bending a steel beam.

I let go of his shoulder and the rabbit slid off the throne. He crashed headfirst into the library table. Along with my messenger bag, the jelly bean jar bounced off the edge of the table and fell onto the cement floor. My messenger bag survived the ordeal, but the jelly bean jar broke into a zillion pieces. Jelly beans scattered all over the place. The bunny bounced twice and flopped unceremoniously face-down into a pile of jelly beans.

The concept of shouting loud enough to wake the dead? Trust me, it's a pile of hot hooey. I didn't need an MD after my name to make this diagnosis. Pedro Conejo was as dead as the proverbial doornail. When the first responders arrive, they're gonna close the swimwear department for who knows how long. This ought to put a nice crimp into Sue Ellen's Easter promotion. And guess who gets to break the good news to Miss Congeniality? None other than yours truly. How lucky could I get?

She's not gonna be a happy camper.

Naturally, I burst out laughing.

Chapter Eight

I called Sue Ellen to deliver the gruesome news immediately after calling nine-one-one. She barked, "I'll be right there." Then she slammed the phone down in my ear. Three minutes later Sue Ellen strode purposefully into the swimwear department alone. She apparently sprouted wings to get down to the main floor of the store from the executive level so quickly. However she accomplished the feat, she didn't use the world's slowest elevator to do it.

I craned my neck searching for Sue Ellen's assistant. "Abby holding down the fort?"

Sue Ellen shook her head. "She's out of the office. Busy trying to replenish our jelly bean supply." Oddly, Sue Ellen didn't so much as glance at the dead rabbit. Yet she tsked her displeasure at the jelly beans scattered all over the floor. "Last night I stayed late to prepare for a management meeting today and replenish the jelly beans supply in the contest jar. When I went to refill the jar, I discovered we had no bags of jelly beans in the office. It was too late to call the candy department buyer or the supplier, and Abby already left for her art class. So, I improvised." She grinned. "Good thing I keep a decent-sized personal stash. I ended up using every jelly bean in the big jar on my desk." She finally turned her head to the Easter bunny's body lying over shattered glass and a bazillion jelly beans. Her smile faded. "Guess we don't need to worry about replenishing the jar anymore."

A dead Easter Bunny lay sprawled across the swimwear department floor. Replenishing the contest jar should only be her biggest problem.

Sue Ellen jutted her chin at the bunny. "Any idea what did him in?"

I shrugged. "No clue. I found him slumped over and tried to wake him. I shook his shoulder pretty hard. I let go of him and he slid off the throne and crashed head-first into the library table."

I held a hand a few inches away from my mouth. "I put my hand over the mouth opening on the costume to see if he was breathing, but it was too narrow for me to tell. I found no pulse, but I'm no doctor."

Sue Ellen spat. "Bet the damned fool drank himself to death."

Carol Compassion certainly has her priorities in their proper order. Geesh.

The cops and EMT team arrived ten minutes after I placed the nine-one-one call. A good-sized crowd of nosy lookyloos gathered around the white fence separating the throne area from the rest of the swimwear department to watch the first responders work on Pedro. Despite their valiant efforts, the Easter Bunny remained unresponsive. Dang. After they separated and interviewed Sue Ellen and me, the older of the two LAPD uniforms who accompanied the EMT team called it in.

Twenty minutes later, a pair of plainclothes detectives showed up. Lead detective Glory Washington's milk chocolate brown eyes twinkled mischievously with recognition as she spied me. Washington and I first met when she was Homicide Detective Miguel Martinez's partner. Now one of the two men in my life, at the time, Miguel was the lead detective on the case when I discovered buying office mogul Bunny Frank's corpse in the California Apparel Mart parking structure elevator.

Always stylishly dressed, Detective Washington is a compact fireplug who wore her close-cropped kinky black hair cut in an Afro and had smooth skin the tone of toasted almonds. Armed with a Master's Degree in Criminology, Detective Washington is blessed with a keen eye for detail, asks probing questions, keeps her head on a swivel, and understands things don't often turn out the way you think they will.

Glory made her way to Sue Ellen and me and offered me her right hand. "Nice to see you again, Ms. Schlivnik. I always figured our paths would cross another time." She grinned elfishly. "Considering your reputation for discovering bodies, it's a miracle it took so long."

I held out my hands in supplication and laughed. "What can I say? It's a gift. It's nice seeing you again too." I turned to Sue Ellen and made the introduction. "Detective, this is Sue Ellen Magee, the buyer for the swimwear department. She'll be able to answer your questions regarding the Easter Bunny and provide any store contact information you need."

The two women sized one another up and shook hands. Then Glory glanced at the Easter Bunny spread-eagled on the floor and shook her head. "Only in LA."

Now a senior detective at the Rampart division under Miguel Martinez as her captain, Glory Washington is the trainer for *Jedidiah-when he's a bad boy to his mama and daddy-Jed when he's not- and Gator to everyone else—Goodwin.* Glory introduced Gator to Sue Ellen and me.

I soon learned through Buddy LaValle, the other man in my life, that Gator and Buddy hailed from the same small town on the other side of the bayou near Baton Rouge, Louisiana, and went all through school together. I'll have to ask Buddy how Gator got tagged with the nickname. Eek. Or maybe not...

According to Buddy, Gator is a stand-up guy, but not the sharpest knife in the drawer. No athletic scholarships were offered to the average jock, and his brains alone proved insufficient to get Gator into college. He went directly into the local police academy from high school. Gator worked his way up to detective the hard way as a uniformed beat patrolman pounding the pavement. After Gator's career stalled back home, his sister-in-law, who works as a police radio dispatcher, encouraged a move west and helped Gator get into the LAPD.

With faded green eyes and thinning dirty blond hair, quasi-redneck Gator is a medium-height and weight guy with translucent pale skin. Slouchy dresser. Ill-fitting, wrinkled off-the-rack suit, loud floral tie not tied right, as though no one ever taught him how to do a proper Windsor knot.

Glory and Gator separated Sue Ellen and me and interviewed us. I had nothing more to add to the information I'd given the uniforms. Since she came in at the end of the movie, all Sue Ellen could give them was the employment details on Pedro Conejo and the contact information of human resources and the store manager.

The detectives made appointments to take our formal statements, handed us business cards, and asked us to call if we thought of anything else before the appointments.

Then Glory and Gator turned their attention to Pedro. They donned surgical gloves and examined the costumed Easter Bunny. The going went slow and tedious and appeared unfruitful. The detectives wisely chose to wait for the medical examiner.

Assistant Los Angeles County Coroner Sophie Cutler and the coroner and CSI teams showed up, and it became another case of Old Home Week. Tall, rail-thin, blonde, blue-eyed, nerdy, and brilliant Sophie Cutler and I have been friends ever since fate brought us together as lab partners in Mr. Hepburn's junior high school biology class. The thought of dissecting a frog made me queasy and Sophie proved incapable of writing a decent essay if her life depended on it. So, we struck a win-win deal. I wrote her papers and she dissected my frog. It's how she got Snip as a nickname.

After bending in half to hug me, the foot-taller Sophie Cutler motioned to the Easter Bunny lying motionless on the floor. "Why am I not surprised to find you in the thick of this?"

Regrettably, this was not my first rodeo. I'd unfortunately discovered several other bodies. As a result, lucky me. I acquired the nickname *Triple M* from the cops…as in the *Mart Murder Magnet*. Merde.

Snip wrinkled her nose. "So, Madame Triple M, I suppose you discovered the body?"

I rolled my eyes. "Nothing gets past you, Doctor Death."

She ignored my dig and smirked. "So, did you

laugh?"

No sense denying it. We've been friends far too long. "You have to ask?"

Snip finger-waved a greeting to Glory standing next to the corpse and tapped my shoulder. "My patient and the detectives are waiting. I'll catch you later. Try to stay out of trouble for a change." I saluted her with the middle finger as she hefted her medical bag and strolled over to Glory and Gator. The three shook hands and the two women burst out laughing as Gator pointed to me. Fanfreakingtastic. Another cop initiated into the *Murder Magnet of the Mart* fan club. Must be my lucky day.

Before I could stop her, Sue Ellen stomped over to the detectives to protest after the two uniforms cordoned off the swimwear department with yellow crime scene tape. "Exactly how much longer are all you people gonna be?" She pointed to Snip and her crew working on Pedro and snapped, "Can't they at least get the stiff out?"

Glory Washington's jaw bunched as Sue Ellen waved to the crowd of lookyloos. "Dead bodies are bad for business. In my world time is money. We're smack in the middle of a big Easter event that has to get back on track *right now* or I'll never hit my numbers."

Chapter Nine

I leaned over the table dividing our booth at Coast Pizza Parlor and swiped a napkin across a glistening glob of red sauce dribbling down Snip's chin. I jealously eyed the ginormous slab of chocolate cheesecake the server set in front of Snip and laughed. "For a medical doctor, your eating habits are atrocious." I tapped my fingers over my heart. "It's amazing your ticker still ticks. My arteries seize just watching you devour that cardiac killer."

Snip shoveled another piece of pizza into her mouth and grinned. She pointed to the last slice of pie on the tray. "Pizza is a perfectly balanced meal. Veggies, carbs, proteins, and dairy all wrapped up in a neat slice." She pointed her fork at the cheesecake and said with a straight face, "It is a medical fact chocolate is healthy…especially for women. I'm a doctor. It's my job to know these things."

I rolled my eyes. "No, your job is to diagnose how your patients ate unhealthy crap like you do that got them dead."

She tsked. "Jealousy is such an unbecoming personality trait. Besides, I run five miles before work every morning as penance for my sins." After finishing off the last slice of pizza, she dug into the cheesecake with a fervor reserved for someone who hadn't eaten in a month. Snip's mommy never taught her the concept of sharing. So, unless I desired a fork tine stuck into my hand, I did not attempt to taste the cheesecake.

I rested my palms on the back of my head and wiggled my fingers. "So, Doctor Death, have you performed the autopsy on the Easter Bunny yet?"

Snip washed down the forkful of cheesecake with a glug of coffee and nodded. "Yes, ma'am."

"So, what is the cause of death?" I smiled hopefully. "Anything simple? A heart attack or natural causes?"

My smile disappeared as she sighed. "I should only be so lucky. The stress on his heart and lungs demonstrated your bunny didn't go off to the big rabbit hutch in the sky too easily. When you found him, he was dead maybe an hour. He wasn't dead long enough for rigor to set in."

Huh? "I'm no doctor, but when I grabbed his shoulder trying to rouse him, he was stiff as an over-starched shirt. So, if not rigor, what did it?"

Snip said, "The stomach contents and tox reports came back today. They, along with the cardiac and pulmonary stress, explained it. We haven't determined yet *what* he ingested as the culprit, but the rabbit died from an extreme case of Botulism."

"Botulism? Like if you eat poison mushrooms?"

Snip donned her professor's cap. "Botulism is a paralyzing nerve toxin, considered to be one of the most potent and lethal substances in the world. It's produced by the bacterium *Clostridium botulinum* and sometimes by strains of *Clostridium butyricum* and *Clostridium baratii*. The rod-shaped bacteria are commonly found in soil and sediments from lakes, rivers, and oceans. The bacteria thrive in low-oxygen conditions, such as canned foods, deep wounds, and the intestinal tract. If threatened, the bacteria form protective spores with a hard coating that allows it to survive for years. The danger is not from the spores themselves, but rather what they produce while germinating. As the *C. botulinum* bacteria grow, they create eight types of neurotoxins so deadly, even microscopic amounts are fatal."

I scrunched my eyes. "So, you're saying our rabbit contracted this, but you don't know how. And it might have been growing in him maybe for years. Did it arbitrarily pick a particular day to kill him or did some sort of process trigger the attack?"

Snip shook her head. "I'm not prepared yet to say exactly how Mr. Conejo contracted the toxin or how long it was in his system. I can say, given the damage to his organs, the toxin amount was substantial and not in his system long. We must investigate the victim's history and interview family and friends to help determine the root cause of his bout."

"What about his history are you looking into?"

Snip steepled her fingers. "His lifestyle might be the key. An outdoorsman? A hiker or a camper? Exposed to contaminated soil or water? Did he consume home-canned foods?"

Snip held up her fingers and counted. "There are five main types of botulism, but we can eliminate Infant Botulism for our vic."

Snip pointed to the pizza crust left on my plate. "Food-borne botulism: *C. botulinum* spores are commonly found on the surfaces of seafood and most fruits and vegetables. The common culprit in many food-borne illnesses is homemade items that have not been properly canned or fermented. Symptoms of food-borne botulism normally begin eighteen to thirty-six hours after ingestion, but it's possible to occur as early as six hours or as late as ten days after eating contaminated food. You cannot see, smell, or taste botulinum toxin— yet taking even a small taste of food containing this toxin is deadly. This type is the probable culprit. The advanced toxin test on his stomach contents will be the telling of the tale as to *which food* is the culprit. Given the long timeframe of symptoms, he could have ingested the toxin up to three days prior and the tainted food would have gone through his system."

Snip picked up a knife and held the serrated edge to her arm. "Wound botulism is another type. If the spores find their way into the body via a wound, especially a deep one, the low-oxygen environment will encourage their growth. People who inject heroin and other drugs are at high risk for this type of illness. It has also been known to occur after serious injuries from car or motorcycle accidents, and even after surgery."

Snip wrapped her arms around her middle and grimaced. "Adult intestinal toxemia is an extremely rare type of botulism in which the spores get into an adult's intestinal tract. It's thought people suffering from gastrointestinal health conditions may be more susceptible."

Doctor Death puckered her lips. "Iatrogenic botulism occurs if too much of the cosmetic form, better known as Botox, is injected into a muscle. Although rare, it occurs when people use knockoff versions of the drug, for example, at so-called '*Botox parties*,' which may not be as carefully prepared as the commercial version. Or if a terrible mistake is made. The lethal dosage of Botulinum toxin is 3,000 units for a 70 kg. adult.

Botulinum is tasteless and odorless—you probably won't know you've consumed the LD-50 of 0.4 billionths of a gram per kilogram of body weight until paralysis sets in.

"Although this is the same toxin causing Botulism, its effects vary according to the amount and type of exposure. For example, Botox is only injected in small, targeted doses. When injected, Botox blocks signals from your nerves to your muscles. This prevents the targeted muscles from contracting, which serves to ease certain muscular conditions and improve the appearance of fine lines and wrinkles. Botox is an injectable drug made from botulinum toxin type A. This toxin is produced by the bacterium *Clostridium botulinum*. This deadly nerve toxin is also the source of Botox, a leading cosmetic solution for wrinkles as well as medical conditions such as migraines and excessive sweating, known as hyperhidrosis. Injecting minute, highly diluted amounts of the toxin into a muscle blocks the nerve signals telling it to contract."

I grinned. "I dunno about this guy and Botox. *Pedro Conejo came to work dressed as an Easter Bunny.* He didn't strike me as the vain type to pump his lips up for better puckering and he was too young for any wrinkle issues."

Snip rolled her eyes. "Because botulism toxin paralyzes muscles, early and classic signs of the illness are drooping eyelids and blurred or double vision, dry mouth, slurred speech, and difficulty swallowing. If left untreated, greater paralysis of muscles of the arms, legs, and trunk of the body will occur, affecting the ability to breathe. We've requested the security film in the swimwear department for the twenty-four hours before and during the incident to see if the victim exhibited any of those symptoms."

I scoffed. "If he didn't take off the head of the costume, you won't see anything."

Snip nodded. "True, but he might not have been able to. Depending on the type of botulism, the length of time in his body, and the amount, paralysis would have come on quickly. The security film will help us build a timeline between when he came on duty at the store, when he first exhibited symptoms, and when you found him. The film may well hold the answers to the question of what killed the rabbit and when."

A vision of the Easter Bunny sliding off the throne and crashing headfirst into the library table made my Thai chicken pizza threaten an encore appearance.

Good grief. I've gotta stop asking questions. Yeah. Right.

Chapter Ten

I related my gruesome discovery to the Yentas and panned the table.

Joan grinned. "Adds a whole new meaning to the expression *the rabbit died*."

Sonia twitched her nose. "So, a guy dressed in an Easter Bunny costume is slumped over on a throne in the Bainbridge swimwear department. You shake him to wake him and he falls face-first into the jelly bean jar and bounces onto the floor."

I nodded.

Sonia grinned. "I'm gonna go out on a limb and bet you laughed your ass off."

No sense denying it. My reputation preceded me. I played a drumroll on the edge of the table with a set of spoons. "Ding, ding. Winner in the first row, ladies and gentlemen. Give the girl a Kewpie Doll."

Joan arched a brow. "And *you* got to give the good news to Miss Congeniality? How lucky can you get?"

I grimaced. "Yep, lucky me all right."

Queenie puckered her lips. "I bet Sue Ellen danced a happy jig. She wanted the rabbit gone and she got her wish."

Sonia pointed a spoon at me. "Your nana used to say…?"

I smiled, relishing the precious memory of Nana's

wisdom. "Be careful what you wish for. Sometimes God punishes us by granting us our wishes."

Hope nodded. "Your nana wasn't just whistling Dixie. Sue Ellen may live to rue the day."

Sonia asked, "So, how *did* the bikini bitch take the news?"

I rolled my eyes. "Exactly as you'd expect. Miss Congeniality stomped over to the detectives to protest as the two uniforms cordoned off the swimwear department with yellow crime scene tape. She demanded to know and I quote: '*Exactly how much longer are all you people gonna be?*' She pointed to Snip and her crew working on Pedro and snapped, '*Can't they at least get the stiff out?*' She motioned to the crowd of looky-loos and said, '*Dead bodies are bad for business. In my world time is money. We're smack in the middle of a big Easter event that has to get back on track right now or I'll never hit my numbers.*'"

Joan quipped. "Guess Carla Compassionate won't be giving the eulogy at the bunny's funeral."

Cut-to-the-chase Sonia sucked in her cheeks. "It may be heartless, but Sue Ellen is right. The Easter promotion is a *huge* part of her business. The same as everything else associated with swimwear, it is a short and sweet, time-sensitive one. She's gotta make hay while the sun is shining, or her profit margin for the whole season is gonna take one heck of a hit."

Joan nodded. "You better believe it. And who is gonna end up paying for her shortfall? Certainly not the bikini bitch." Joan pointed an index finger around the table. "Who do you think? *All of us.*"

Hope widened her eyes. "With Pedro out of the picture, who knows if anyone else is capable of running his company? It won't be easy to replace forty Easter Bunnies if Pedro's company folds." She played a ta-da with her hands. "No bunnies, no Easter promo."

Queenie poked her index finger into her cleavage. "Well, if Sue Ellen thinks all her swimwear vendors are gonna take up the slack, she's got another thing coming." She surveyed the table and jutted her jaw. "I won't speak for the rest of the suppliers, but they haven't minted enough money yet to get *my derriere* into one of those bunny costumes."

I waved the notion off with a flick of a wrist. "Don't get your bloomers in a bunch. Rent-A-Rabbit is a big company. A successor provision must be in place if something happened to Pedro."

Sonia asked, "Any idea how long Sue Ellen's department will be closed?"

Joan's smirk dripped sarcasm. "Out of respect to the dearly departed, surely until after the bunny is buried."

I rolled my eyes. "Hardly. Once Snip's team bagged Pedro's body and the coroner's team wheeled him out of the store, the CSI team collected the broken glass and all the jelly beans into evidence bags. They wrapped the throne and the pieces of the library table in plastic and sent everything to the lab. Glory and Snip said their teams should be finished performing the physical examinations of the area by today." I glanced at the clock hung on the wall behind the barista's station. "If they keep to that timetable, they'll remove the yellow tape and release the department by the end of the day. If the Bainbridge floor setters have extra props available, the department should be up and running by tomorrow. I'm going over to Sue Ellen's later today to confirm some deliveries and I'll get the lie of the land."

****

I got to the arch at the entrance to the Bainbridge swimwear department a little after three. I screeched to a stop to pick my jaw up off the floor. If I hadn't been in the department the day before, I'd never guess twenty-four hours earlier a guy seated on a throne dressed in an Easter Bunny costume keeled over dead. The yellow crime scene tape draped around the department had been removed, and with one exception, everything else was in place exactly as the day before the debacle.

The one difference? Every stitch of Ditzy Swimwear sat on a markdown rack with a prominent sign advertising all styles fifty percent off the regular price. The immediate goods we shipped to Bainbridge filled the four-way rack in place of Ditzy's suits. Good thing Sue Ellen banned Michael Chennault from the store. He'd birth a cow.

I almost peed myself when a menacing male voice behind me sneered in my ear. "Admiring your handiwork?"

I counted three Mississippi's to get my heart beating normally and turned to face him.

Sparks of rage crackled thunderbolts in Michael Chennault's evil eyes. He pointed to my swimsuits now occupying the rack formally his and spat. "Apparently, you paid no attention to me. I warned you not to take advantage of my situation. Now you're going to pay."

The arrogant jerk is such a moron. As if I had *anything* to say over the way Sue Ellen stocks her floor.

His eyes followed my index finger as I pointed to the security cameras flanking the ceiling over the swimwear department. "Big brother is watching you, so, if you're considering anything involving bloodshed, you might want to rethink your plan." I tsked. "You showed up after Sue Ellen warned you not to, so you didn't learn to follow instructions either. Trust me, this is *not* the way to get back into Sue Ellen's good graces." I angled my head to the exit. "Get your ass outta Sue Ellen's department while the getting is good."

He waved an index finger under my nose. "Better look over your shoulder. I'm not finished with you." Without an ounce of irony, he announced as he stalked toward the exit, "No one tells Michael Chennault what to do. No one."

****

The dumbstruck Yentas sat slack-jawed as I recapped my visit to the Bainbridge swimwear floor the day before.

Once I finished, Joan was the first Yenta to remember how to speak. "Lemme get this straight. Michael Chennault *threatened you* on the floor of the Bainbridge swimwear department?"

I nodded. "Yeah, he did."

Hope sighed. "My God, the man has lost his mind."

Sonia asked, "You two alone in the department or could someone overhear him?"

I shrugged. "I dunno. Mid-afternoon, so I imagine some customers were on the floor. To be honest, I was so focused on Michael, I never looked around."

Joan held out her hands. "This Easter gig is a *huge,* chain-wide promotion. Some customers *must* have been in the department."

Queenie tapped her index finger on the tip of her nose. "You're damned lucky he threatened you in such a busy place and not in a less-occupied spot."

I shivered recalling several of my past altercations

with bullies in the bowels of the mart subterranean parking structure.

Hope gulped. "I'd take his threat seriously. Since Sue Ellen threw us out of the store, Michael's behavior has been completely irrational. He's blaming anyone and everyone except himself for the mess we're in. He is laser-focused on revenge against anyone *he thinks* did this to him."

I squared my shoulders. "I'll do my best to steer clear of him, but I won't allow him to dictate the way I run my business or change my life to suit him." I widened my eyes. "Believe me, I'm not his problem. Sue Ellen was not the least bit amused after I described the incident. She has both the motivation and the power to bury him in the industry. I did some fancy tapdancing and held her off this time, but if Michael continues pissing in Sue Ellen Magee's hat, he's gonna regret it." I pinched my index finger and thumb close together. "She is this close to dropping the hammer on him."

Chapter Eleven

I scooped the last piece of pizza from the tray onto my plate, and from the intensity of Snip's glare, you'd think I'd snatched the slice right out of her mouth.

Before I cut into it, I asked, "So, any progress determining how Pedro got botulism poisoning?"

My favorite coroner arched a brow. "You betcha." Snip pointed to the purloined pizza slice and flashed an evil smile. "And if you wanna know, it's gonna cost you."

I rolled my eyes and slid the plate across the table. "Extortion is so demeaning."

Her response? She hacked off half the slice and shoved it in her mouth. She washed it down with a glug of Chardonnay and daintily patted her greasy lips with the corner of a sauce-stained napkin.

She batted her eyes. "You're not gonna believe it, but honestly, we coroners can't make this kind of stuff up."

I wiggled my nose and chomped my front choppers. "Poisoned carrots?"

Doctor Death anchored her index finger over her thumb. "Close, but no cigar. The rabbit died from tainted jelly beans."

Whoa. Now she had my full attention. "Holy cow. The manufacturer shipped tainted jelly beans. "Any other reports of botulism poisoning from the jelly beans?"

Snip shook her head. "Nope. Only the one Bainbridge case."

I whistled low. "Man, Bainbridge will go after the supplier big time. Such a huge lawsuit will probably put Teenie Weenie Jelly Beanie out of business. Does Glory Washington have the report yet?"

Snip nodded. "Yeah. I faxed it to her this afternoon."

I grinned. "I'd pay good money to be a fly on the wall when Glory gives the good news to Sue Ellen Magee." I laughed. "Poor Glory. Talk about killing the messenger. I wouldn't be surprised if we heard Sue Ellen yelling all the way to the mart."

Snip shrugged. "The manufacturer is not at fault."

I slapped my cheeks. "Are you saying the jelly beans were *tampered*?"

Snip nodded. "Yep. If the botulism grew organically, the source of the poison would be in the interiors of the jelly beans."

"Then how did the jelly beans get tainted?"

"The exteriors were coated over by Botox. Pedro Conejo was murdered."

Holy guacamole.

****

If they opened their mouths any wider, the Yentas' jaws would have hit the table.

"Yep. You heard it right. Pedro Conejo consumed jelly beans *purposely tainted* by botulism poison."

Hope asked, "And your friend the coroner is *sure* the jelly beans were not shipped tainted from the supplier?"

"Positive. The interiors of the jelly beans were poison-free, but the exteriors were coated with Botox."

Hope narrowed her eyes. "How does it prove the jelly beans were not shipped tainted from the supplier?"

"Snip explained if the jelly beans were tainted organically, the interiors of the candy are the location of the poison. They weren't. Someone coated the exteriors of the jelly beans with Botox."

Sonia tapped her lower lip. "Well, now it all makes sense."

Queenie asked, "What does?"

Sonia said, "I happened to be in Sue Ellen's office late yesterday afternoon when the two detectives arrived along with two uniformed patrolmen and a search warrant."

Hope held out her hands. "Looking for…?"

Sonia played a ta-da with her hands "Jelly beans."

Hope scrunched her eyes. "Jelly beans. Nothing else?"

Sonia shook her head. "Nope. They bagged, tagged, and confiscated every container of jelly beans in Sue Ellen's office, the outer office, and the two storage closets."

Joan snorted. "Good gravy. Sue Ellen is addicted to them. The Queen of Mean sans her jelly bean fix? I bet she pitched a fit."

Sonia shrugged. "Detective Washington didn't give Sue Ellen a chance to react. She handed Sue Ellen the warrant and ordered all of us to wait in the hallway of the buyer's cube while the police conducted the search. We stood outside the office for an hour or so. Then Detective Washington came out into the hallway and said we could go back in. She handed Sue Ellen a stack of receipts for everything confiscated, and the police left taking everything they collected."

Joan drummed her fingers on the edge of the table. "Makes no sense. Sue Ellen eats jelly beans from those canisters every day. If they were contaminated by botulism, she'd be as dead as the bunny."

I tapped my index finger on my lower lip "Maybe that was the point of searching her office. If the police suspect Sue Ellen, they came to the same conclusion."

Queenie nodded. "Right. If they are able to place her at the scene of the crime with the tainted jelly beans, she is toast."

I gulped. "If the security tapes film the swimwear floor from the time the store opens to closing time, Sue Ellen is screwed. She told me *she personally* replaced the jelly beans Pedro ate during the day from the contest canister the night before the bunny died. The cops are gonna say she coated a portion of her jelly beans with Botox and put them in the contest canister to poison the rabbit."

Sonia scrunched her eyes. "Even if she wanted to murder Pedro, how on God's green earth did Sue Ellen get her hands on Botox?"

Hope puckered her lips out. "Maybe she went to one of those Botox parties you hear about and helped herself to some of the product when no one was looking."

Joan burst out laughing. "And you see *Sue Ellen Magee* at one of those hoity-toity parties rubbing elbows with the princesses of plastic surgery? If you do, better get your eyes checked because you don't see too good."

Sonia shook her head. "Nah. It's easy to buy it on the internet."

I scrunched my eyes. "I dunno, girls. The Queen of Mean is a gold medal nasty ballbuster, but a murderer?" I shook my head. "She might have *wished* the bunny bit the dust, but do the deed? Not in a million years. A bully like her? The fact of the matter is she doesn't have the stomach for it. She almost wet herself just being in the same showroom as Lissa Charney's corpse hung in the closet. Sue Ellen practically pole-vaulted out of the Royal Swimwear showroom when Detective Yakamura finished questioning her. The truth? When the rubber meets the road, Sue Ellen Magee is all foam and no beer."

Joan bunched her shoulders. "If not Sue Ellen, who punched the bunny's ticket?"

Queenie tapped her index finger on the tip of her nose. "Who had the most to lose?"

Sonia arched a brow. "Better yet, who had nothing *left* to lose?"

Hope and I locked eyes. "Michael Chennault."

Chapter Twelve

"Good aftanoon, Miz Magee. Sorry to interrupt you, but we're gonna need a few minutes of your time."

Detective Goodwin's lazy drawl meandered his words as slow as a sated alligator crawling across a bayou floor. His voice filtered out from Sue Ellen's office into the hallway and stopped me mid-step into her outer office. I plastered my body adjacent to the doorjamb and angled my head perpendicular to the wall to see into the room and still not be seen by them. I leaned in as far as possible and cocked an ear. Glory Washington stood next to Gator, but the lead detective let Goodwin do all the talking.

Sue Ellen glared at the two cops and fanned her desk covered by files and folders. "As you can see, I'm up to my neck in work." She made a sour face. "Since you came without an appointment, get to the point and make it snappy. I've got a deadline to meet."

Gator ignored Sue Ellen and laid a sheaf of papers in front of her with a flourish of his hands.

Sue Ellen jutted her chin at the documents. "What's this?"

"A copy of the lab report on all them jelly beans and the canisters we confiscated from your office." Gator smiled a languorous smile and tapped the papers with a bony index finger. "Take a gander. Whaddya think the test results are?"

Sue Ellen snapped like a cranky croc. "The *only* possible result. Not one tainted jelly bean."

Gator agreed. "Right as rain, ma'am, except…"

Impatient Sue Ellen rudely cut the cop off. "So, your little witch hunt wasted your time and mine." Sue Ellen waved her arrogant dismissal with a casual flick of a wrist. "I appreciate your giving me the information, but you could have called and not come all the way across town to personally give me the good news." Sue Ellen glanced at the clock on the wall and pointed to the door. "I've a staff meeting to attend in fifteen minutes I need to finish preparing for, so if we're finished, show yourselves out."

I put a fist to my mouth to prevent laughing out loud as Gator stared Sue Ellen down and flexed his fingers. Did the cop plan to put his hands over Sue Ellen's mouth to shut her up or slap her silly? Instead, Gator rolled his eyes and sighed. "It would be mighty helpful, ma'am, if you'd quit flappin' your jaws long enough to lemme finish. As I started to say before you interrupted, all the jelly beans tested negative and every container and canister tested clean…*except one.*"

Gator pointed to the empty spot on the top right corner of Sue Ellen's desk. "The inside of that specific container was coated with enough Botox to plump up the lips of a small army." Gator rolled his shoulders. "Since you didn't croak after touchin' it, I guess you musta worn gloves or sumpthin'."

Sue Ellen's eyes bugged. "Are you outta your mind, Detective?"

Gator solemnly shook his head. "No, ma'am, I'm not."

Sue Ellen poked her thumb into her cleavage. "If you're implying that *I* had anything to do with Pedro Conejo's death, then you're crazy."

Gator pointed to the lab report. "I'm not *implyin'* a darned thing. I'm statin' a *fact*." The cop smiled, but the smile never reached his eyes. "I'm afraid, Miz Magee, you're gonna miss attendin' the meetin'."

Sue Ellen slammed a fist on the desk so forcefully the jelly bean-shaped paperweight anchoring the stack of folders bounced across the blotter and hit the floor. She sneered. "And why, Detective Goodwin, will I not be attending the meeting?"

Gator shrugged. "Because, Miz Magee, the thing of it is, we viewed the security film of the night before Mr. Conejo died, and we witnessed *you*, ma'am, fillin' the candy jar next to the throne with jelly beans." He pointed to the empty place on Sue Ellen's desk "And you filled it by transferrin' the jelly beans from that *particular canister* to the jar on the library table." Gator smiled, displaying a set of blindingly bright white choppers. "The same tainted jelly beans sent the Easter Bunny to the Lord the next day."

Gator held his hands out and framed them the way a movie director sets a scene. "The security tape told the whole story. The next frame showed Mr. Conejo drinkin' out of a flask just before the store opened. Then he shoved a huge fistful of them jelly beans down his piehole." Gator snorted a laugh. "I'm guessin' by the amount of candy he helped himself to, either the bunny was a jelly bean fiend or he downed the candy to disguise the liquor smell on his breath. The next frame showed the Easter bunny walkin' to the throne. The last frame he's sittin' on the throne and keeled over dead."

My heart skipped a beat as two LAPD uniforms arrived. They stepped into Sue Ellen's office once Glory Washington gave them the signal with a slight nod of her head.

Gator solemnly said, "Sue Ellen Magee, you are under arrest for the murder of Pedro Conejo."

My mouth opened wide enough to catch a family of flies.

The detective held out his hands and raised them palms faced up. "Stand up and put your hands behind your back nice and slow and easy. Now don't be fussy and create a scene, and go makin' this more difficult on yourself than it already is. Understand this, ma'am. Either way, you're comin' with us."

White as a ghost, Sue Ellen trembled from head to toe, and stumbled as she numbly complied to Gator's command. The older of the two uniforms kept his right hand on his service revolver as he took a card out of his shirt pocket with his left. He read Sue Ellen her rights while the younger one unclipped a set of handcuffs from his utility belt. I flinched at the ominous click of the metal bracelets as they locked Sue Ellen's wrists into place.

Sue Ellen is no killer, yet Gator laid out a helluva compelling case. How in the world would Sue Ellen get herself out of this hot mess? Certainly not on her own. Unfortunately for Sue Ellen, the expression what goes around comes around reared its ugly head. After all the years her suppliers endured her abuse, would the swimwear industry rise to the occasion, or let the bitch of bikinis drown? I made a snap decision and prayed for divine intervention.

The two uniforms sandwiched Sue Ellen between

them as they marched her perp-walk style toward the outer office door. I blocked their passage and ignored Glory Washington's searing glare. I laser-focused on Sue Ellen's eyes widened to the size of coasters by fear.

"Sue Ellen, do you have a lawyer?"

She shook her head.

My knees knocked loud as an untuned car engine, but for Sue Ellen's sake, I swallowed the quiver in my voice. "Okay. No problem. A criminal attorney will meet you at the police station." I cupped my ear. "Listen carefully." I twisted my index finger and thumb together like an invisible key locking my lips. "*Do. Not. Utter. Another. Single. Word.*" I pointed to Glory and Gator. "No matter what they say, the threats they make, or what they do, *do not react*. Keep your mouth shut until you meet with your attorney. Do you understand?"

Her eyes filled as she nodded. She mouthed thank you as I stepped aside and let the terrified prisoner and her police escort pass.

****

Word of Sue Ellen's arrest flew through the industry with the speed of a rocket. The following morning, I muscled my way through the mob crowding the newsstand next to the mart deli and bought a copy of the *West Coast Apparel News*.

I distributed their coffees to the Yentas and laid the newspaper in the center of the table. The headline above the fold screamed "*Bainbridge Bikini Buyer Behind Bars.*"

The mood at the Yenta table was subdued as I relayed the sordid details of Sue Ellen's arrest. She would never win a congeniality award, but the buyer we all loved to hate a stone-cold killer? Nah. Not in a million years. Now proving it? Another story.

Saucy Joan slapped the table. "Thank the Goddess Sue Ellen signed all my purchase orders before they cuffed her and took her away."

Always practical Sonia mused, "All kidding aside, who *is* gonna handle the department while Sue Ellen is in the slammer?"

I said, "I spoke to Abby this morning. Sue Ellen's arrest will not create any interruption of business. Management put Abby temporarily in charge. She has full authority to review products and write orders."

Sonia tapped her lower lip. "Sounds as if management has already passed judgment on Sue Ellen…"

Hope shook her head. "Not necessarily. Management has no idea how long before Sue Ellen will be back, or *if* she's coming back. Their business goes on with or without Sue Ellen."

Hope asked, "Is anyone representing Sue Ellen?"

Queenie smirked. "You mean is anyone *willing* to represent her?"

I shrugged. "Ms. Markowitz. Who else?"

Joan widened her eyes. "After all the crap she's pulled, you actually *helped her* get a lawyer?"

"Sue Ellen Magee is a gold medal champion jerk, but she is our jerk. It looks bad, yet in my heart of hearts, she didn't do it." I grimly surveyed the Yenta table. "Sue Ellen is up to her eyeballs in trouble. She's as ornery as a mule yet Sue Ellen's no more a murderer than any one of us."

Sonia grinned. "Ms. M. finally met her match. After a few sessions with her new client, the old girl might consider retirement."

No kidding.

Sonia didn't have a lawyer when she was wrongly arrested for buying office executive Bunny Frank's murder. I called my Uncle Barry, a personal injury attorney in Beverly Hills for help, and he recommended Ms. Markowitz. *"If I ever found myself in trouble with the law, Rose Markowitz is the one attorney I'd ever call."* With complete trust in my uncle, I put Sonia Wilson's life in Ms. Markowitz's capable hands. The diminutive octogenarian criminal defense attorney extraordinaire saved Sonia Wilson's ass. Hopefully, she'll do the same for Sue Ellen…if Ms. M. doesn't strangle her pain in the patootie client first.

Sonia asked, "Did you and Ms. M. meet?"

"Yes. We met last night, after she interviewed Sue Ellen."

Joan laughed. "The old gal ready to punch your lights out?"

I grinned. "Not yet. Thank the Goddess Ms. M. loves a challenge."

Queenie pursed her lips. "Good thing. Gator Goodwin laid out one helluva strong case."

Analytical Sonia tapped an index finger on her lower lip. "At first glance, it looks as if Sue Ellen's goose is cooked. The police certainly had enough to arrest her, yet there's no smoking gun."

Hope's eyes bugged. "Are you out of your mind? The security film showed *Sue Ellen* transferring the tainted jelly beans from the canister she kept on *her* desk into the contest jar."

Sonia shrugged. "And? The police are hard-pressed to prove *Sue Ellen* is the one who coated the jelly beans with the poison and put them in the canister on her desk."

Queenie saluted Sonia with her coffee cup. "You're right. Sue Ellen is a lot of things, but stupid isn't one of them. She knew the security film would show her transferring the jelly beans from her canister to the contest jar. If she was going to poison the bunny with tainted jelly beans, she'd never put them in her own canister."

Sonia wagged a finger. "Right as rain. *Anyone* could have coated the jelly beans with the poison and put them into Sue Ellen's canister to frame her."

"Ms. M. agrees with you. The case against Sue Ellen is circumstantial at best, but Ms. M.'s fear is a jury would be swayed by the security film." I wrung my hands. "Let's face it, Sue Ellen is not going to come across as a sympathetic defendant."

Sonia patted her cheeks. "Good grief…just imagine *her* on the witness stand?"

Joan arched a brow. "A jury would convict her the minute she opened her mouth."

Sonia clasped her hands as if in prayer. "Thank the Goddess defendants in criminal trials can't be compelled to give testimony or be cross-examined."

Hope pinched her brow. "And she didn't exactly keep her feelings about the bunny a state secret. Remember, the bunny is the reason her promotion is off the table."

Queenie sighed. "And there's an industry cast of thousands who would love to see her spend the rest of her life behind bars."

I said, "The bunny messed up her promotion, but Michael Chennault is the one who has the biggest axe to grind. Michael's product line got thrown out of the most important account in the city because of Sue Ellen. It could create a domino effect, and she'd de facto put him out of business." I played a rat-ta-tat-tat with a spoon on the edge of the table. "My money is on him. He threatened to get her fired or *see her dead*. He didn't get her fired…maybe he tried to get her dead. The guy keeps questionable company. Is it hard for him to get his hands on the poison? Not hard at all. Say he coats the jelly beans with the poison before he sends the gift pack to Sue Ellen."

Hope shook her head. "Abby said she hid the gift pack."

I pursed my lips. "Doesn't mean she didn't restock Sue Ellen's canister with those jelly beans when Sue Ellen wasn't around to see who they came from."

Queenie narrowed her eyes. "So, you're saying Michael intended to murder *Sue Ellen*, and the bunny got poisoned by accident?"

I grinned. "You betcha."

Sonia widened her eyes. "How are you gonna prove *that* and avoid getting yourself dead?"

I smiled evilly. "By getting Mr. Chennault to prove it for me."

Hope aimed a teaspoon at me like a gun. "Michael Chennault is a vicious, vindictive bastard who will stop at nothing to get even. He has the resources to do it, and wouldn't lose a minute of sleep over taking you out."

I jutted my jaw. "Michael Chennault is nothing more than a well-dressed thug. He's an arrogant bully. And arrogance will kill you every time."

Queenie narrowed her eyes. "Don't go doing anything stupid. Stupid is the way you get dead."

I grinned. "No more girls nights out with you and Snip together. You two are starting to quote one another's lines."

Chapter Thirteen

Saturday night Siggie got invited to a sleepover birthday party for my friend AJ's King German Shepherd, Peso. AJ is married to Buster Schumansky, the local sales rep at Ditzy Swimwear. Buster and I worked together during my stint as the Vice President of Ditzy. AJ is also an LAPD homicide detective and Miguel is her Captain.

AJ is responsible for Miguel and me first getting together and she hoped our burgeoning romance would lead to something permanent. AJ "asked" Siggie to spend the night. Her way of giving Miguel and me some extra uninterrupted time alone.

Miguel and I dropped Siggie and his overnight bag at AJ's mid-afternoon and headed downtown to spend the rest of the day and evening at historic Olvera Street. Considered the birthplace of Los Angeles, Olvera Street housed the oldest buildings in the city. Now a major tourist attraction, it featured a variety of trendy restaurants, strolling Mariachi bands, as well as funky souvenir shops, and ethnically-oriented art galleries.

We took our time in the art galleries and admired the works of two up-and-coming local artists. One painted haunting scenes of the hardscrabble life in the barrio and the other uplifting portraits depicting hopeful signs of change.

We left the last gallery and strolled hand in hand at a leisurely pace, bobbing and weaving between the crowd. We stopped in all the shops carrying Mexican arts and crafts. Miguel insisted on buying me a gorgeous bright, multi-colored embroidered peasant blouse in a floral design from a charming clothing boutique. After shopping all the stores and covering the length of Olvera Street, we'd done a fair amount of walking and were famished. We stopped to read the menus outside of many eateries and ended up at Joaquin Santos. With a well-deserved reputation for serving the best street tacos this side of Tijuana, Joaquin's small stall is always busy, and Saturday was no exception. We waited our turn in a long line that snaked out the door and halfway down the street—and worth every minute of the wait.

It was a Chamber of Commerce kind of a beautiful day featuring temperatures on the mild side and not a cloud in the sky, so, we took our food and margaritas and ate at an open-air picnic area adjacent to the bandstand while Mariachi bands serenaded us. We ate in companionable silence and took in all the sights and sounds.

We finished our meal and my heart rate increased to warp rate when Miguel turned to me and cradled my hands in his. Miguel looked into my eyes and cleared his throat. The normally smooth-as-silk Captain stuttered shy as a teenager working up the courage to ask a girl to the prom. "I-I've g-got s-something i-important to-to a-ask y-you."

Good gravy…was he *proposing*? We'd been dating for some time now. We weren't exclusive, but until Buddy came back into my life, Miguel and I weren't dating anyone else. Miguel and I were still in the seeing if this will work out stage—not the to death do us part stage. Well, at least one of us isn't. Yikes. And if Miguel and I didn't already have enough obstacles to overcome, adding Buddy to my love life complicated my relationship with my favorite police captain to the max.

I steeled myself and gulped. "Okay, ask…"

"My older sister Adela's youngest daughter Isabela is turning fifteen. Fifteen is a special birthday for girls in our culture and we celebrate with a type of coming-of-age party. The best way to describe it? Sort of a cotillion mixed with a Bar Mitzvah party, if you squint. The celebration is called a Quinceanera or the fiesta de Quinceanera, quince años, fiesta de quince años, and quinces. It is a celebration of a girl's fifteenth birthday. It has pre-Columbian roots in Mexico from the Aztecs and is widely celebrated by girls throughout Hispanic America. It is a huge event and a highlight for both the birthday girl and the whole family. I am Izzy's godfather, so of course I play a big role." Miguel took a big gulp of air and gave me an expectant look. "Izzy's Quinceanera is next month, and I would be honored if you would accompany me to the party." He smiled. "It's about time I introduce you to my family. They've heard so much about you, it's as though they already know you. So…?"

Since he didn't get down on one knee holding an engagement ring, I almost fainted with relief. I care deeply for Miguel, but above and beyond the complication of Buddy, the good Captain and I have some potential deal-breaker issues that might be insurmountable to overcome.

Since our first encounter, Miguel received two promotions and is now a Captain. We started seeing one another right after his last promotion. Regrettably, I have a habit of discovering corpses. Needless to say, Captain Martinez is not a happy camper when I stick my nose into their cases after his detectives arrest the wrong suspect. With Glory Washington as the lead detective on the Easter Bunny's murder and her arresting Sue Ellen, it is just a matter of time before I interfere in Glory's investigation and Miguel and I butt heads. Could our relationship survive another conflict? Slimsky to nonesky in my book. Only time will tell.

Miguel didn't propose marriage, yet this invitation certainly propelled our relationship to another level. A level I wasn't yet comfortable with. I grew dizzy from the game of mental ping pong going on inside my head. Was I ready to meet his family? What did my accompanying him to this hugely important family affair indicate to him? To his family? To me? Was accepting the invitation a tacit agreement to a more serious relationship? Would Miguel now expect to meet my family? A vision of Mike Schlivnik interrogating Miguel made me just two steps shy of crazy. And let's not forget Buddy. What in the Sam Hill do I do about him?

What to do? What to do? Maybe Miguel might not mind too much if I yanked out my cell phone and called Queenie for some advice? Nah. Time to pull on those big girl panties. I drained the last dregs of my margarita to buy myself a few beats to think. Then a voice sounding remarkably the same as mine said, "I'd be honored to accompany you."

Crap on a cracker. What the hell did I just get myself into? Well, too freakin' bad. No do overs for this one. It's done and no undoing it now. I barked a nervous laugh to disguise my panic attack. "This being my first Quinceanera, I might need some fashion advice for an appropriate dress."

Miguel grinned from ear to ear and yelped, "Fantastico!" He pulled me up from my chair and danced me around the table in a crazy quilt sort of polka. Miguel came back down to Earth and released me. He picked up our stacked trays. "While I'm returning the trays, may I interest you in a refill on the margarita?"

After accepting a party invitation I wasn't prepared for, I could have downed a whole pitcher all of my own, but I smiled and shook my head. "Tempting, but I'd better pass. I may fall asleep before the jazz concert starts and it'll be hell waking me."

"In that case, I'll drop off these trays and grab a couple of coffees. Molinillo de Café is next door to Joaquin's. This coffee shop does some unusual blends." Miguel grinned, flashing a set of dazzling white teeth.

"I hate to burst your bubble, but when it comes to coffee, I am a strict traditionalist. I drink it straight—the way nature intended it—strong and black."

Miguel held out his hands. "Okay, I get it. Just this once try something different. I bet you like it. They grind only coffee beans from Mexico and blend them with interesting combinations. My favorites are coffee blended with dark Mexican chocolate or coffee blended with cinnamon."

I rubbed my chin. "Okay. Just this once. Which one do you recommend?"

"They're both delicious." Miguel snapped his fingers. "I'll get one of each and we can share."

I clapped and smiled. "A perfect solution."

Miguel made a two-fingered salute and pushed his way through the throng of people crowding the narrow street.

The whole party conversation exhausted me. I turned my seat to face the sun and closed my eyes. Suddenly, a blast of icy cold air came out of nowhere and chilled me to the bone. I pulled my lightweight jacket tighter around my shoulders and cocked open an eye to see why the temperature dropped fifty degrees. I almost peed myself as two spinning swirls of freezing air, one around five inches taller than me and the other the height of a toddler, spun counterclockwise like twin tornados. My eyes bugged as they morphed into apparitions, and sat down on either side of me. The taller ghost was Marie LaValle. The smaller one was her daughter, Justine. The other man in my life, Buddy LaValle, tragically lost his wife Marie and young daughter Justine when they were both killed in a horrific wrong-way-driver crash on Interstate 10 in New Orleans several years ago.

Marie pointed to Miguel's disappearing backside and huffed with righteous indignation. "Land sakes alive! It's about damned time. We've been floatin' around this place for hours. I never thought he'd leave."

I shook my head like a wet dog to clear the cobwebs. Good grief. *How much booze was in the margarita*? If one has me hallucinating, thank the Goddess I declined a refill.

Justine shook a little finger at Marie. "Mama, you said a bad word!" She giggled. "Gonna wash your mouth out with soap."

I craned my neck, looking for Miguel. Cripes, he better hustle back with the coffee, and pronto and go right back for more.

I shivered from head to toe as Marie blew a puff of freezing cold air in my face to make her presence undeniable. "Pay attention, girlie. We don't have a lot of time to waste on pleasantries." She waved an arm toward Miguel and pursed her lips. "What in the Sam Hill are you doin' with *that man* when you're supposed to be with *my Buddy*? You think I pushed Buddy all the way out to LALA land and far from home for you to be with *other men*? You need to get with the program and fast, honey chile."

I poked a finger in her arm to see if she was real, but my hand went right through her and came out frozen. Eek. I sure hope the java is strong...and one cup is never gonna be enough.

Marie sucked in her cheeks. "You don't know spit about apparitions, do you?"

I shoved my frozen hand in my armpit to thaw it out and asked, "Does Casper the friendly ghost count?"

Marie tsked. "Clearly not. Well, it don't matter none." She pointed to Justine. "We cain't move on until we're sure Buddy is gonna be okay."

I tapped an index finger in my chest. "And this has what to do with me?"

Marie rolled her eyes. "For some reason or another, Buddy made it sound like you had a good head on your shoulders...but I dunno. You seem a little slow on the uptake, so lemme spell it out for you." She pointed to Miguel walking back balancing a couple of coffees and a basket full of dessert churros on a tray. "You simply cain't continue seein' this other guy. It's outta the question. Not if you're gonna marry Buddy."

My eyes bugged. "*Marry Buddy*? Who put a notion like that into your head?"

Marie sighed like she carried the world on her shoulders. "You must be blind as well as dumb. Don't you see the way my Cajun boy looks at you? He makes the same goo-goo eyes at you he made at me when we was courtin'." I blushed from head to toe when Marie tapped her index finger on her lower lip. "I've seen the way you look at him too. A blind guy could see you're head over heels in love with him. An' don't try denyin' it either."

Good gravy. The ghost of Buddy's wife *spying* on us? Yikes. Imagine if we'd been…you know…? Oh. My. Goddess. Those street tacos flipped a loop-de-loop in my tummy and threatened to make an encore appearance. This must be either the booze talking or my imagination running wild, right? I forced myself to calm down. Yet, I answered a ghost… I pursed my lips. "You're the one who is blind, not me. Buddy still wears his *wedding ring*. Not a day passes when he doesn't say '*Gee, if only Marie could see me now*.' You been to his house?" I pointed to Marie and Justine. "The place is a shrine to your memories. Buddy might have moved across the country to start over, but he brought you two along. I won't deny I have feelings for him. I do. But I can't…no, I'm not willing, to compete with the ghosts of his dead wife and daughter. It's a contest I'd never win, so forget it."

Justine protruded her adorable lower lip and tightly hugged the same kind of doll made out of fabric swatches sitting on Buddy's desk. "*Please* marry my daddy. I don't want him to be alone and always so sad. Since he cain't have me, I want him to have another little girl to love."

I opened my mouth to reply, but the two ghosts disappeared into thin air as Miguel put the tray laden with coffee and churros down on the table. I jumped when he touched my shoulder. My hand shook as I took the steaming cup of coffee from him. His concerned eyes searched mine. "Are you all right? You're sheet white and look like you've seen a ghost."

You don't know the half of it, Mickey.

I plastered a wan smile on my kisser. "I'm fine. Just trying to figure out the appropriate attire for a nice Jewish girl to wear to a Quinceanera?"

Not sure Miguel bought the pile of crap I was selling. Luckily for me, the first Latin jazz group jumped on the stage and the saxophonist broke into his version of *El Gaucho*. The cut is one of Miguel's all-time favorites. Miguel was mercifully occupied for the next two hours lost in the Latin beat and, thank the Goddess, asked no other questions I had no answers to.

As for me? I fought a losing battle trying to pay attention to the concert…too distracted by the events of what should have been a relaxing day, yet remarkably turned into anything but. First, a party invitation that instantly catapulted my relationship with Miguel to who knows the next level, and then an encounter with two matchmaking ghosts. Merde.

All of a sudden, I'd gone from no man in my life to too many men in my life. Maybe Siggie was the only man I needed in my life.

Chapter Fourteen

After four long encores, the jazz concert went way overtime. Given the ever-present traffic on Interstate Ten going west, we didn't get back to the marina until after eleven o'clock. The street tacos and churros were mere fond memories and we were both hungry, yet didn't want anything heavy late at night. Miguel parked his SUV in one of the guest spots in the Porto Paloma Marina subterranean garage. It was a balmy night for the beach and we walked to Harry's Hideaway. Harry's is a locals late night dive at the end of the Washington Street pier that serves the best appetizers, desserts, and drinks in the city and features a honky-tonk piano player who is seemingly able to play any song the audience requested. Between the din of the crowd and the music, it was difficult to have a conversation. Thank the Goddess for small favors. My head spun from the day and my reservoir of words had dried out.

We beat the crowd by leaving twenty minutes before last call and headed back to the marina. Miguel folded me into the crook of his arm as I shivered when an onshore gust of cold wind pushed us along…or were Marie and Justine chaperoning? I dragged my eyes surreptitiously up and down the street and breathed a sigh of relief. Mercifully, Miguel and I appeared to be alone.

Miguel wrapped his muscular arm tightly around my shoulders, and I snuggled into the comfort of his warmth. The biting wind gusted again and we stepped up our pace. At a faster clip, we made it a short trip to cross Admiralty to Palawan Way and the entrance to Porto Paloma Marina. After a ten-minute walk, we arrived at the security gate of my basin.

Miguel rubbed his hands together. "It's amazing how much the weather changed from the time we pulled into the garage and now. It's twenty degrees colder. If I'd known, I would never have suggested walking to Harry's." He pointed to the stairwell at the parking structure. "No need for you to stand out in the cold waiting for me. Open the gate and let yourself in and give me the key. Then you get aboard your boat. I'll grab my overnight bag from the car and meet you."

I opened the gate, yet kept the key in the palm of my hand. I'd never earn a living as a poker player. Nothing got past the detective as his eyes searched mine. I looked away, but he put his finger under my chin and gently turned my head around. "Something's going on with you. You're normally chatty as a magpie, but you've hardly said a word all night."

I squirmed and found something utterly fascinating about my shoes.

His eyes widened. "It's the party, isn't it? You don't want to go, do you?"

I had to say something, but what? Do I explain two matchmaking ghosts to a cop? Yeah, right. And two minutes later end up in the loony bin for observation. I looked him in the eye. I owed him that much. "It's not that I don't *want* to go…"

"Then what is it?"

"It's more like *should* I go?"

He squinted. "I don't understand?"

I bunched my shoulders. "It's a big step. One I'm not sure I'm ready to take."

"Do you want to keep seeing me?"

"That's the hell of it. I do."

His eyes twinkled. "Your nana used a clever way to help you decide on something, right?"

I rolled my eyes. "Draw a line down the middle of a piece of paper and make me list the pros and cons."

He played a ta-da with his hands. "The party is next month, so you've some time to decide. Give it some thought and let me know the week before. I don't want you to feel pressured to do something you're not comfortable with. I'll be okay whichever way you choose." He leaned over and kissed the top of my head. "For tonight, I'm gonna go home and give you some space."

Without uttering another word, he turned and crossed the street. I stood rooted to the spot until he disappeared down the stairs to the garage.

Chapter Fifteen

I spent a sleepless night pacing the length of the houseboat trying to figure out what-or who-I wanted in my life. As dawn broke Sunday overcast and chilly, I still had no clue. The good news? No encore visit from my ghostly matchmakers. Thank the Goddess for small favors. Since getting any shuteye appeared out of the realm of possibilities, I headed over to AJ's to collect my hound.

I showed up at AJ's bungalow alone at eight o'clock sharp with a dozen right-from-the-oven Nosh N' Nice bagels, a tub of cream cheese, and a six-pack of A Jolt of Java's high-test blend. I braced myself for a whole lot of yappy barking and a canine collision greeting, yet none came. I craned my neck to look out the kitchen window to the back yard. "Awful quiet. Did Buster take the pups down to the beach for a run?"

AJ nodded. "He took them for an early morning romp on the Venice Beach boardwalk at dawn. The pups are probably napping after their workout. You just missed Buster. He dropped the boys off in the back yard twenty minutes ago and headed to the Central Valley for the rest of the week." AJ gave me a wonky once-over after she leaned around me looking for Miguel and came up empty. "Good grief. The boss dropped you off and he's *still looking* for a parking space?"

I shook my head and said I came alone.

She grinned "I never figured the good captain as one of those love 'em and leave 'em kind of guys."

Her grin faded when I said, "Don't ask…"

Of course, my curious cop compadre couldn't resist. I related the Quinceanera story between bites of bagel and glugs of coffee but wisely left out the two ghosts. AJ fixed me with a look of pity and shook her head. "That's it? A *party invitation* twisted your panties in such a bunch?"

I clucked my tongue. "Not just *any* party. This one is Cinemascope and Technicolor with his whole family checking me out like a prized steer at an auction." I held out my hands in supplication. "I'm not ready for the meet the family gig yet."

AJ aimed a half-eaten piece of bagel at me like a pistol. "Don't screw this up, Holly. Miguel Martinez is as fine a man as it gets. And for some inexplicable reason, the guy is crazy for you."

We finished our breakfast in awkward silence. After bussing my dish and coffee cup, I thanked her for inviting Siggie to Peso's party and collected my hound.

****

I put the top down on the convertible and took the long way home paralleling the ocean on Main Street trying to clear my head. Between the lack of a good night's sleep and the uncomfortable conversation with AJ, I found myself out of sorts. I didn't want to go home and mope, but couldn't come up with anyplace else to go so, Siggie and I got back to the marina around ten. The early morning overcast burned off and the sun shone bright in a baby blue sky. We took a leisurely stroll to the Washington Street pier and walked one lap around our marina. As we made the turn to our side of the basins, I caught a glimpse of a buff guy sporting a Captain's hat out of my peripheral vision stepping over the bow of a forty-four-foot cabin cruiser onto the dock. Michael Chennault grinned evilly and gave me a two-fingered salute as he came up the gangplank. He opened the security gate and speed-walked to catch up with me.

Michael jauntily tipped the brim of his hat. My blood ran cold as he chirped like a robin celebrating the first day of spring. "Top of the morning to you, *neighbor*." He pointed to my side of the marina. "Your houseboat is on the other side of the marina at basin seventeen hundred, right?"

Michael's friendly tone of voice was as smooth as a newborn baby's tush but his angry eyes flashed daggers as he waggled his fingers toward Siggie. "That's a stately-looking dog." The fur on Siggie's back stood on edge and he growled deep in his throat when Michael bent to pet him. I wrapped a protective arm around Siggie's neck as Michael pulled back and smiled. "You must have to leave him alone a lot while you are at work. With all these big power boats and lots of people around, the marina can be a dangerous place for pets. Better keep an eye on this handsome guy. Be a real shame if something happened to him…"

I've a clown car full of cops in my life, so why isn't one ever around when I need one? My knees turned to jelly and knocked like an untuned engine as Michael and I locked eyes for one terrifying moment. After such a delightful encounter, the rest of the day went by in a blurry train wreck.

****

The Yentas sat in stunned silence the next morning

as I related my encounter with Michael.

Hope's eyes bugged as she slapped her cheeks. "My God! The lowlife *threatened* Siggie? Did you call Miguel? Did he arrest Michael?"

I tsked. "Call Miguel and say arrest one of my boat neighbors for being concerned for my dog's safety?"

Hope snapped, "Horsepucky. Michael didn't mean it that way and you know it."

I pursed my lips. "Michael didn't threaten Siggie. He just said the marina is a dangerous place for pets and it would be a shame if something happened to Siggie. He's right, it can be dangerous for animals."

Joan panned the table. "Holly's right. Michael covered his ass by choosing his words carefully. He made a veiled threat, and one that should be taken seriously."

Sonia clucked her tongue. "Should she bring Siggie to work?"

"Why not? He'd be great entertainment for buyers." Joan smirked. "Or the muscle to ensure they write their orders."

Queenie rubbed her chin. "All kidding aside, Michael's threat is no joke. How *are* you going to protect Siggie?"

"Obviously, taking him to work is not a viable solution. But I won't leave him alone on my boat any more either. I've enrolled him in doggie daycare Mondays, Wednesdays, and Fridays. He likes the place and it's a safe environment. The two gay guys who own the place put strict security protocols in place. And my neighbor, Muriel Lobowsky is crazy for Siggie." I laughed. "She considers him the grandson she always wanted and is thrilled to take him for the day on

Tuesdays and Thursdays."

Hope asked, "You do a lot of traveling for work. And then?"

I held out my hands. "The same thing I already do now. If it's a long trip, I check him into The Barkingham Palace Doggie Hotel on Sepulveda. If it's just an overnight trip, he either stays at Muriel's or AJ and Buster's."

Joan mused, "Beyond hiring a private security guard for Siggie, how much more can you possibly do?"

I jutted my jaw. "If so much as one of Siggie's whiskers is out of place I will go gunning for Michael. He better pray I don't catch up with him. And I promise you, I will. And when I do, I guarantee I will make him pay. And go to the bank on this…It won't be pretty."

Chapter Sixteen

Saturday was another Chamber of Commerce gorgeous kind of day. Mild temperatures, a gentle breeze to tickle your fancy, and not a single cloud blemished the robin's-egg blue sky. Around nine-thirty Siggie and I made our way up the gangplank and crossed Palawan Way to the subterranean parking lot across the street from our basin. I dropped the top down on the convertible and belted Siggie and myself in.

I cranked up the radio volume on the oldies station and we sang along with the Beach Boys as we traversed the Marina Freeway. Miraculously, the 405 was comparatively empty as we merged into the fast lane and headed north into the San Fernando Valley.

Forty-five minutes later, I parked in front of Milton Albin's Stamp & Coin World. We stood in front of the store entrance and I ruffled Siggie's furry head. "Are you ready to see your BFF Mr. Albin?" Siggie danced a little two-legged jig and barked two short woofs I took as a yes, so, I opened the creaky metal-framed glass door. I breathed in the slightly musty smell of canceled stamps and as though time stood still, I reverted back to an awkward junior high school girl.

I've been an avid philatelist since I was a teen. What is a philatelist? It's a fancy word for a stamp collector. My introduction to stamp collecting was with a birthday gift of an album filled with stamps from one of my mother's cousins. The pictures, colors, and shapes of the stamps in the album fascinated me. But beyond licking one and attaching it to an envelope to mail, I didn't know anything else about the hobby. A coin and stamp store was next to the take-out pizza place my mother frequented a few miles from our house. I took the album to the shop to see if the proprietor would teach me about stamp collecting. The first time I walked into the store, a magical world opened up for me and turned into my lifelong love affair with stamps.

Generous, knowledgeable, and patient Milton Albin, the proprietor of the stamp and coin shop, looked up when the bell over the doorjamb jingled. His face broke into a broad grin as we stepped inside the store. Slightly stooped over with age, a bespectacled, wiry, balding Milton Albin excused himself to a customer and came around the counter. He wrapped his arms around me and then held me at arms-length. "Holly Schlivnik...you're a sight for an old man's eyes." He shook a gnarled index finger at me. "When you were a young girl, you rode your bike to my store every Friday after school and bought stamps with your allowance...and now? It's been way too long since your last visit."

I smiled indulgently. "Mr. Albin, regrettably, since I am now running a company, I don't have as much free time as I used to. And I do a lot more traveling in my job. Even so, it hasn't been too long since my last visit. Don't you remember? I was in the store only three weeks ago to order the last two 1893 Columbian Exposition commemorative stamps I need to complete the set. You called a few days ago to say you had a pair in mint condition and it's the reason why I'm here today."

Before Mr. Albin responded, Siggie decided he didn't cotton to be ignored. He stuck his wet, cold nose into Mr. Albin's hand and made his presence known. Mr. Albin bent at the knees and scratched behind Siggie's ears. "Sigmund, my dear friend. So rude of me to not greet you!" Mr. Albin turned sideways and pointed to a man standing at the counter. "Once I finish working with the gentleman over there and then your mommy, you and I will play too. Is that okay?" Siggie barked his approval.

My heart seized as I took measure of Mr. Albin. The years had taken a toll on him. Deep wrinkles creased his face and the little left of his hair turned steel-wool gray. Yet thankfully, he was the same twinkly-eyed man sporting an elfin smile. He still wore the same type of knit vest over a chambray shirt haphazardly tucked into loose-fitting chinos. Scuffed penny loafers still shod his feet. The familiar jeweler's loupe and a magnifying glass he used to evaluate the condition of a stamp or coin still hung on a lanyard around his now mottled neck.

Mr. Albin spun me around and we faced the big, burly, middle-aged man standing at the counter leafing through a stamp catalog. "Darren," Mr. Albin grazed my right shoulder with his fingertips. "Where are my manners? I apologize for not introducing you to one of my earliest customers."

I extended my right hand to the imposing man whose baseball glove-sized hand swallowed mine. He smiled and spoke in a gravelly voice as though he gargled with razorblades. "Darren Flynn. Nice to meet you, uh Ms....?"

"Holly Schlivnik. Nice meeting you too, Mr. Flynn."

Flynn shook his head and smiled. "Call me Darren. Mr. Flynn is my father."

Siggie barked and Flynn laughed. He bent down and pumped Siggie's extended paw. "The pleasure is all mine, Sigmund." Flynn turned to me and asked, "As in Dr. Freud?"

I nodded. "Yep. One and the same. Siggie is my confidant and part time psychiatrist." I grinned. "I tell him everything. My hound can keep a secret."

Flynn jerked his chin to Mr. Albin. "So, you've been coming to Albin's Coin & Stamp for quite a long time?"

I nodded. "Since I was a young whipper-snapper as my grandpa Charlie used to call me. Mr. Albin was a wonderful teacher who taught me the way to properly handle and evaluate the quality of stamps. He suggested for a novice collector like me, the best way to learn about stamps was to buy the canceled ones, instead of those costlier ones in mint condition." I grinned. "Good thing too—canceled stamps were all a pre-teen's allowance could afford. I still have my original world stamp collection, but now, I only collect US uncanceled stamps."

I pointed to the wall behind me. "My visits to Mr. Albin's store always began at the huge wall and all those envelopes containing canceled stamps clipped onto it. After making my selections, I'd bring my envelopes to Mr. Albin to ring up. He opened the envelopes, and carefully took the stamps out using a pair of tongs, and that's when the magic began. He had a story for every stamp, and his vivid descriptions made the stamps come alive. No matter the stamp's story, he told it like a novel with a beginning, a middle, an ending, and a point of view. He told each story his special way; taking his time, slowly building up to the cliffhanger, and dramatically pausing right before the climax. Talk about pacing and the way to build tension to the finale. Mr. Albin had it down pat. He conducted my tour of weekly adventures around the world and through every era of history with stamps in every color and shape imaginable serving as the tickets for the ride."

Darren grinned. "He hasn't changed a bit. He still has a story for every stamp. On each visit I make to see Milton, I always stay for a couple of hours so as not to miss his spiel."

Mr. Albin blushed red as a ripe tomato from his face to the top of his balding head. He tapped a bony finger on his chest. "Holly, must I keep reminding you? You're a grown-up now. Call me Milton, for crying out loud."

I turned my eyes downward and scuffed the toe of my deck shoe into the worn linoleum. "Sorry. I've tried. I just can't do it." I looked up at the old man and shrugged. "It doesn't sound right when I say it."

Mr. Albin rolled his eyes.

I affectionately patted his arm. "No matter how old I get, you will *always* be Mr. Albin to me."

Darren waved a meaty paw toward the busy street. "You still live in the neighborhood?"

I shook my head. "I haven't lived in the valley since I went away to college. I'm in the marina. I live on a houseboat."

Darren's eyes lit. "Wow. Such a cool way to live. Are you in the boating industry?"

I laughed. "Not even close. I'm a sales exec in the rag business. And you?"

Darren said, "I own a used car dealership on Van Nuys Boulevard south of Sherman Way." He asked,

"Are you a manufacturer's rep?"

I said, "I started my career as a rep and now I am in management." I proudly puffed out my chest. "I am the President of Mermaid Swimwear. I split my time between the Apparel Mart and our executive offices downtown."

The color drained out of Darren's face. "*Swimwear*." He spat it out as though it was a dirty word. He growled. "So, you must work with the *Magee bitch*."

Good grief. Had Sue Ellen bought a car from the guy and given him a strong dose of her blue-ribbon attitude? I narrowed my eyes. "Did Sue Ellen buy a car from you?"

Darren snorted a laugh and threw up his hands. "Perish the thought. She and my wife went through the executive training program together at Bainbridge Department Stores. After they graduated, they were both up for the swimwear buying position. My wife scored the highest of the graduating class and had the inside track for the swimwear job until an unfounded rumor of Lois taking bribes spread around. It was a filthy lie and Lois was exonerated, but she lost out on the job to Magee. Lois is sure Magee spread the rumor. Even though she was proven innocent, Lois got sent to purgatory as the candy buyer and has been stuck in the candy department ever since."

I shivered at Darren's pure evil laugh. "What goes around comes around. If there is a God, Sue Ellen Magee will rot in jail for the rest of her life." Darren smiled. "Lois has an interview with human resources this week. By the time you and I run into one another again, Lois will be the swimwear buyer and justice will finally be served."

I bent backward to look the guy in the eye. "Sue Ellen Magee is one helluva pushy pain in the patootie, but she's no more a killer than I am."

Darren's murderous glare threatened to cut me in half when I said, "The cops arrested the wrong person and I'm gonna prove it."

Chapter Seventeen

Monday morning the Yentas sat on the edges of their seats as I shared the details of my run-in with Darren Flynn.

Hope lasered me with an incredulous stare. "So, you think this *Flynn woman* set Sue Ellen up and is the real person who poisoned the Easter Bunny?"

No-nonsense Sonia tsked. "Come on, Hope. It's one helluva leap to make from being pissed at Sue Ellen for beating her out of a job to setting her up for murder!"

Chastened, Hope surveyed the table. "Okay, maybe she didn't set Sue Ellen up." Hope waved a teaspoon in my direction. "From the way her husband related the story, the woman *was* ready to kill Sue Ellen. Who's to say she didn't try? Maybe she *meant* to poison Sue Ellen, but Sue Ellen didn't cooperate by not eating the poisoned jelly beans. Instead, Sue Ellen refilled the ginger jar in the swimwear department with the contaminated jelly beans and the rabbit died after eating the candy from that jar."

Queenie tapped an index finger to the tip of her nose. "Maybe Holly's on to something. Mrs. Flynn *is* the candy buyer, so she has the means."

Joan pursed her lips. "She has the means, but the opportunity…? No problem getting the jelly beans, but getting them inside Sue Ellen's office and into her candy jar on her desk? The buyers must lock their offices at night, don't you think?"

I grinned. "If there's a will, there's a way." I glanced at Queenie and laughed. "Maybe Mrs. Flynn borrowed an end-around ploy from our burglary playbook and gave the night watchman or the cleaning crew some cock and bull story about her leaving something in Sue Ellen's office after a co-op meeting regarding the Easter event and they let her into the office."

Queenie sniffed with righteous indignation. "Oh no you don't, sister. That's *your* burglary playbook, not mine."

I batted my eyes. "Oh, yeah? You do the crime; you do the time."

Sonia tapped a spoon on her coffee cup. "Let's not get hung up on the opportunity right now. Let's focus on the means and motive. Without that, who cares about the opportunity?"

"You're right. Let's see if Lois Flynn passes the sniff test." I took a notepad and pen out of my messenger bag. "She has access to jelly beans and maybe to Sue Ellen's office. Her motives? Jealousy and revenge." I pinwheeled my arms. "We've seen suspects with a lot less motive who turned out to be the killer."

Joan asked, "And the botulism? She can't go into the supermarket and buy some."

Sonia rubbed her pointy chin with an index finger and thumb. "True. Maybe she attended one of those Botox parties and stashed a dose or two in her purse?"

Queenie said, "Maybe a friend who is a dermatologist or a relative who is a pharmacist?"

Hope scrunched her eyes. "Or she's a patient of a dermatologist who prescribed Botox for her."

Sonia said, "She could buy it on the internet."

Joan pursed her lips. "And you're gonna find that out *how*? You can't exactly call her up and ask her."

I played a hand ta-da in Queenie's direction. "Looks like we're going on another Schlivnik adventure."

Queenie smirked. "Not me, sister. I told you the last time. My burgling days are over. But just for giggles and squeaks, do you have a brilliant plan to get into her office? You don't have a key. You don't work at the store, so you don't know the security or janitorial staff."

I held my hands out in front of me. "So? I'm a vendor who left something critical in her office and I ask to be let in." I shrugged. "If it's not broke, don't fix it. It worked before, why not now? As my dad taught me, if you act like you know what you're doing, people assume you do."

Queenie funneled her lips. "Security and the cleaning crew don't start their rounds until after the store closes. You planning to hide in the ladies' room until the store closes?"

I clucked my tongue. "I bet the cleaning crew starts at the top and works their way down. They clean the executive suites first and then the lower levels. I'll call and give some BS excuse and find out what time they start. It's probably way before the store closes. I'll also find out the time Mrs. Flynn usually leaves for the night."

Queenie shot back, "And let's say for argument's sake all goes as planned for this cockamamie stunt, any ingenious plan for getting out of the store? Or are you sleeping on one of the floor sample mattresses in the furniture department?"

I toasted her with my coffee cup. "A fantastic idea! We'll go to the lingerie department and grab a couple of nightgowns first." I laughed. "Get real. You've been to the Bainbridge buying cube. Those offices are not huge. It'll take the two of us fifteen minutes tops to go through her office."

Queenie nodded. "It won't take *the two of us* any time." She poked an index finger into her cleavage. "Because I am *not*, repeat, *not* going on this destined-for-disaster misadventure of yours." She sniffed. "Somebody's gotta be available to bail you out of jail."

I shook my head. "Such a wuss. Where's your sense of adventure?"

Queenie grinned. "At home keeping my sense of self-preservation company."

Chapter Eighteen

Five minutes before noon the next day I stood adjacent to the Ditzy showroom entrance with all the caution of the bomb squad. I leaned around the corner and breathed a sigh of relief. Hope was the only one inside. Thank the Goddess. I needed another run-in with Michael Chennault like I needed a migraine.

The bowl of oatmeal at breakfast was a distant memory as I crossed the threshold. Crap on a cracker. Hope held a half-dozen samples in the crook of her arm. I'm famished and she's preparing for an appointment. Business always comes before pleasure, but my time is as valuable as hers. So, why didn't she call to cancel our lunch date? I tamped back the annoyance squeezing my gut.

My stomach growled a complaint as I held up my watch and waved it at Hope. "Good grief. Don't tell me you're going to an appointment *now*. I'm starving."

Hope waved me off as she pulled her purse out of the top drawer of her desk. "Don't get your knickers in a knot. I'm only going downstairs to the Bulletin Buying Office and dropping off these samples for a style-out. If there isn't a long line to check the samples in and get a receipt, I'll be maybe twenty minutes, tops."

I swiped the back of my hand across my forehead and headed for the door. "Okay. I'll meet you downstairs at the mart deli and get a table. If you don't get a table before the crowds arrive the lunchtime wait might be at least an hour."

Hope brushed aside my suggestion with a flick of a wrist. "Do me a favor and wait for me in the showroom. I'm expecting a package of fabric swatches for an appointment tomorrow. If no one's around to accept the package, the delivery person will leave a note. The trouble is their customer service won't guarantee the time tomorrow I'd receive the re-delivered package."

I wrinkled my brow. "Fine, but if they don't arrive by the time you're back and we leave for lunch, won't you still have the same problem?" I gulped. "Or is Michael coming up to the showroom? You said you can set your watch by him. The factory might be on fire, yet he is out to lunch daily at eleven-thirty and up to the showroom promptly at twelve-thirty. If he is, I'm gonna pass on lunch with you today. I don't want to risk another altercation."

Hope moved her index finger back and forth like a metronome. "Michael is out of town the rest of this week. He left at the crack of dawn to his storage garage in the valley to flatbed a race car." Hope checked her watch. "By now he is halfway to the Laguna Seca Raceway in Central California to meet his pit crew and prepare for a big race over the weekend." She coughed to conceal a nervous giggle. "Thank the Goddess. Any more of his bellyaching about Sue Ellen and I'd either have to kill him or quit my job."

I said, "I'm relieved Michael is far away, but your fabric swatch delivery is still an issue if we go out. Do you want me to order in? If I do it now while you're at the buying office, lunch should be delivered by the time you come back."

Hope shook her head. "Buster said he'd be here in time for us to go to lunch and for the rest of the day. If you don't mind, I'd prefer to go out." She leaned in to whisper conspiratorially. "I've got something to discuss, but not in the building. The walls in the mart have big ears."

Okaaaay. A bit too cloak and dagger for my taste. Maybe she's a mystery buff? At the risk of hurting her feelings by laughing, I resisted whispering back. I flexed my index fingers and thumbs like chopsticks. "Are you in the mood for Chinese food? The Blue China Moon Café always has great lunch specials."

Hope shook her head. "I love The Blue China Moon, but it's too close to the mart. The place will be crawling with nosy garmentos. Do you like Korean food? Park's Diner from Koreatown just opened a second location on Spring Street between 9th and 8th. It's not a long walk and I bet no one from the mart ever heard of it. And their Korean barbeque is the best this side of Seoul."

"I've never eaten Korean food, but I'm game to try something new." I pointed to the door. "Now get going already. My tummy is growling so loud I'm surprised you don't hear it."

Hope waved goodbye and ran for the elevator. I settled into a chair at the far workstation and looked around. It was weird being back as a visitor to a place I once worked at.

No changes in the layout since the time I worked for Ditzy. Hope and Buster's desks still sat next to one another at the front of the room. My old desk and now likely Michael's sat in the far back corner. The desk angled out to face the front of the showroom, yet far enough away to allow for a modicum of privacy.

My eyes had a mind of their own and curiosity got the best of me. I gave a cursory look outside the hallway and casually sauntered to my old desk. I slid into the worn leather seat cushion and checked the time on the clock hanging on the wall behind Hope's desk. She'd been gone five minutes. I calculated twelve minutes the most to go through Michael's desk. I pulled the handle on the center drawer, but nothing doing. Mental head slap. The damned drawer always stuck. I smacked the underside of the drawer sharply, using the heel of my left hand. I grimaced as the drawer opened with a squeak as loud as a toy mouse.

I foraged around the drawer but nothing out of the ordinary caught my eye. Two packs of sugar-free gum, a *half-empty* pack of condoms—eek—too much information! Two bucks' worth of loose change, and the usual assortment of pens, paper clips, and scratch paper.

I focused my attention on the three drawers on the side of the desk. The top drawer held a stack of line lists, color catalogs, and blank order books. The middle drawer was separated by hanging dividers each housing fat files of Ditzy's biggest accounts organized by volume, not alphabetically. The Bainbridge file should have been the fifth one from the front but it was missing. Curious.

I bent down to open the lower drawer, and surprisingly found it locked. I opened the center drawer and searched for the key. Unless Michael took it, the key should still be inside a paperclip box tucked in the back left corner of the drawer. I reached into the back and pulled the box out of the drawer. Eureka! The trusty key sat on the bottom of the box hidden by all the paperclips.

I inserted the key and turned it to the right. The lock clicked open.

More folders. This time Michael's personal and financial files. I glanced at the clock. Eight minutes left. I opened the camera app on my phone and took pictures of every document in the files. The Bainbridge file was the last one in the back of the drawer. I pulled it out and photographed every page from the date I left the company to the present. I finished and tried to put the files back, but something got stuck and they didn't all fit in. Crap. I folded myself in half and bent over. I angled my head sideways into the drawer to find the item gumming up the works. I smacked my head on the top of the drawer as I pulled a file labeled "*S.E.M.*" marked in red stuck between the back of the drawer and the top where the drawer slid back in. Time check. Two minutes. Maybe I'd get lucky and Buster or Hope would be late. As if. The curiosity was killing me, but I didn't have the luxury of time to go through the file. I photographed every page, put them all back in the right order, and returned all the files to the drawer. I locked the drawer and buried the key in the paperclip box. Just as I pushed the box back into the corner and slid the center drawer closed, Buster strode purposefully into the showroom.

Buster glanced at me still seated at Michael's desk and deadpanned. "If you're angling to get your old job back, from the way Michael cusses every time he hears your name, I don't think it's gonna happen."

I squirmed in Michael's chair. I patted the arm and choked out a nervous laugh. "Old habits die hard."

Buster's bushy eyebrows shot to the top of his receding hairline. Apparently, I wore as my mother called it, "*my lying face*."

Hope returned and stopped short seeing me seated at Michael's desk. I jumped out of the chair as if my pants caught fire and grabbed my messenger bag. I practically pole-vaulted out of the room and called over my shoulder. "Good to see you, Buster. Tell AJ I'll call her tomorrow to make plans to get together."

Hope speared me with an incredulous look as I spun her around like a top and strong-armed her out the door. We pushed our way into the packed elevator and got off in the mart lobby. We strolled along Main Street in companionable silence. While waiting for the light to change at 6th Street, Hope slid her eyes over to me. "So, did I give you enough time to find whatever you were looking for in Michael's desk?"

I barely caught myself as I tripped on an uneven stretch of pavement. "What on the Goddess's green Earth are you talking about?"

Hope tapped her cleavage with an index finger and smiled indulgently. "Remember me? We worked together in that showroom eight hours a day, five days a week, for over four years. I *know* the way you think." She stared me down with an expectant look. "Cut the crap and quit wasting time. They call it lunch *hour* for a reason. So, spill it, sister."

We crossed the street and I batted my eyes. "You *gave* me enough time?"

She clucked her tongue. "Yeah. No other vendors checked their samples in for the style-out, so I finished my business in no time. I spent the next fifteen shooting the breeze with Daisy, the swimwear buyer's assistant, who checked me in." Hope grinned. "I *knew* you'd go through Michael's desk looking for...I don't know. I figured you'd need some time to do it. So, did you find anything?"

She nailed me. No sense denying it. I shrugged. "I dunno know yet. I didn't have enough time to go through the files and cherry-pick the important documents, so I took photos of everything that struck me as important. One in particular got my attention. The file was labeled *S. E. M.* and the only name written in red ink."

"Oh my God!" Hope's hands flew to her cheeks. "Michael has a *file* on Sue Ellen?"

I nodded. "It sure looks that way. I shudder to imagine what I'm going to find."

Hope funneled her lips. "Expect the worst. Michael Chennault is a nasty, vengeful thug capable of inflicting unimaginable pain."

An involuntary shiver traveled the length of my spine as Hope opened the door to the restaurant and motioned me to follow.

****

After the busboy cleared our table, Hope reached into her purse and pulled out an envelope. She turned it around to face me and laid it on the table.

"A present?"

Hope used a chopstick to point at the envelope. "Kinda. This is a key to Michael's garage in the valley as well as the alarm code instructions. The stuff in his showroom files might be incriminating, but if a smoking gun exists, I guarantee you, it's stashed in his racecar garage."

Hope never struck me as the cat burglar type. Still…

My tone bordered on incredulous. "You managed to *make an extra copy* of his key and alarm code?"

Hope clucked her tongue. "Hardly. He *gave it to me* in case of an emergency or if he was out of town and needed something."

"Why you? Seems pretty odd he'd entrust something so valuable to an employee. Why not his wife or his brother-in-law? Someone he trusts?"

Hope smiled sardonically. "Michael doesn't trust *anyone*. Why me? Because I'm the one he thinks would do whatever he says to do and ask no questions." She shrugged. "Arrogant Michael operates under the theory that nothing is as lasting as a relationship based on fear. And since he sees himself as a powerful man to be feared, he naturally assumes I am afraid of him." Hope pushed the envelope to me and grinned evilly. "So, I'm the last person on the planet he'd ever think had the guts to disobey him, let alone betray him…"

Chapter Nineteen

Queenie and I grabbed a bite at Herbie's Old-Fashioned Burgers located diagonally across from the south entrance to Bainbridge Department Store. Herbie's is an iconic downtown landmark operating continuously twenty-four hours a day at the same location for fifty years.

We finished our messy yet scrumptious feast, pushed our way out of the crowded twenty-table dive, and jaywalked across the street to Bainbridge's. I checked the time as we approached the Easter event arch leading into the swimwear department. "We're almost a half hour early. Abby is probably still out to lunch. Let's go through the department and check out our second delivery of the jelly bean bikinis on the new floor display."

We crossed under the arch and headed to the four-way rack adjacent to the fenced-off area housing the Easter Bunny. We reached the mannequins decked out in our jelly bean bikinis and Queenie squealed like a hunting hyena. She pointed to a woman holding a clipboard standing across the aisle. "OMG! I don't believe it. See the redhead holding the clipboard? She's the one wearing a ruffled blouse over animal print capris and the feather boa around her neck."

I followed Queenie's index finger with my eyes. "I

see her. Who is she?"

"Dixie Chandler." Queenie sighed. "I always wondered what happened to her."

Queenie broke into a clumsy run with her feet strapped into her signature sky-high four-inch stilettoes and raced to the woman's side. My jaw dropped as Queenie yelled out Dixie's name and spun her around. At first, Dixie's eyes narrowed with annoyance. Then they widened with recognition and her expression morphed in a nanosecond from exasperated to euphoric.

The two women threw their arms around one another. They created entertainment for a few curious customers in the department as they danced a little jig between the four-way rack and the mannequins while screaming each other's names. I arrived on the scene as the two women stopped dancing and held each other at arm's length. They burst out laughing when the crowd gave them an appreciative round of applause.

Queenie tapped her cheeks. "Dixie Chandler... where *the hell* have you been all these years? It's like you disappeared into thin air after graduation."

Dixie twisted her lips into a wry smile. "It's a long story..."

Before she began telling her tale, I cleared my throat to get their attention. I took a defensive step back as Dixie glared at me like I was an uninvited guest who crashed a teenager's slumber party. Queenie pulled me to her side and gushed her embarrassment. "Good gravy. Holly, I'm so sorry...I completely forgot my manners. Dixie, meet my business partner and dear friend, Holly Schlivnik. Holly, Dixie and I were thick as thieves in the same class at fashion school." Queenie grinned at Dixie and giggled like a naughty girl. "That we graduated after all the stunts we pulled is a miracle…"

Dixie grasped my extended right hand and covered it with hers. She smirked. "We two rebels were a baaad influence on the rest of the class." Dixie winked at Queenie. "Yet the two top students in our class, so Doctor uptight Dean Williams couldn't throw us out of the school like he wanted to." She laughed. "I bet he and his cohort the Missy Prissy fashion trends professor Adamson celebrated for a week after we received our diplomas."

I glanced at my watch. Twenty minutes before our meeting. I pointed to Dixie's clipboard. "Do you work at Bainbridge?"

Dixie nodded. "Yes indeedy. I've been working at the store for almost four months. Before I came to Bainbridge, I was the fashion and trends director at Milgram's Department Stores in San Francisco. When Allied Stores bought Milgram's, they consolidated a lot of positions. I'm one of the lucky ones. An opening became available when the Bainbridge fashion and trends director retired right before the Milgram sale was finalized. They gave me the choice to transfer to Bainbridge and not be let go like so many others." She pointed to the Easter Bunny's throne. "This event was my first major assignment." Queenie and I looked at one another as Dixie spat out the words like watermelon seeds. "And thanks to that bitch, Sue Ellen Magee, it was almost my first and last."

Dixie pointed to the four-way rack featuring our swimsuits. "Are you swimwear vendors?"

Queenie fingered the jelly bean bikini on the mannequin. "As a matter of fact, yes. This is one of our suits."

Dixie scrunched her nose as if she'd just taken a whiff of a baby's poopy diaper. "So, you have the *pleasure* of working with Sue Ellen. Please accept my condolences." She turned a one-eighty around the swimwear department and sneered. "What goes around comes around. And Sue Ellen Magee got hers." Dixie gave Ms. Magee a round of applause. "Couldn't happen to a more deserving person."

****

The next morning Queenie and I related our encounter with Dixie to the other Yentas.

Hope furrowed her brow. "She *really said* Sue Ellen's arrest for murder *couldn't happen to a more deserving person?*"

I nodded. "Oh yeah. She practically bared her teeth as she said it."

Hope pursed her lips. "Boy, that is harsh."

Joan looked over the rims of her glasses and gave Hope the kindergarten teacher look of disapproval. "Why does this come as any surprise to you? Let's face it. Sue Ellen Magee will *never win* the Miss Congeniality award."

Hope lifted a shoulder. "It's not a surprise. Sue Ellen rubs everyone wrong one way or another, for crying out loud. And she will spend the rest of her life in jail if Miss M. doesn't pull a miracle out of her magic bag of tricks."

Sonia asked, "So, this Dixie had a run-in with Sue Ellen over the Easter event floor setup?"

Queenie pursed her lips. "It was much more than just a run-in. As the fashion and trends director, it is Dixie's job to develop the theme for these types of events and create everything from the department decorations to the fashion show, contest, and giveaway based on the current direction the market is heading. Sue Ellen rejected everything Dixie put together and went over her head to management to get her way. According to Dixie, Sue Ellen compared Dixie's abilities to her predecessor and questioned Dixie's competence for the position to the Vice President of Fashion. She tried her best to get Dixie fired."

Joan quipped, "Maybe Dixie's problem is she doesn't share Sue Ellen's love of jelly beans."

Queenie said, "Dixie created an innovative, sophisticated, on-trend retro theme featuring swim styles from the past as the focal points of the displays and a tribute to the famous Easter parade down Fifth Avenue in New York as the fashion show routine." Queenie clucked her tongue. "Quite a departure from the *jelly beans on drugs* theme Sue Ellen insisted on."

Joan raised her eyebrows. "An understatement of epic proportions."

Hope shrugged. "I dunno. Call me stupid…I love the way Sue Ellen decorated the swimwear department for her event. After all, what's Easter without jelly beans?"

I said, "I thought Sue Ellen's department looked great too. However, Dixie's rendition sounded spectacular."

Sonia tapped her lip. "You said Dixie came from Milgram's in San Francisco, right?"

Queenie nodded.

Sonia glanced around the table. "Any of you ever sell to Milgram's?"

Five shaking heads indicated no.

Sonia asked. "Why not?"

Joan said, "Milgram's was on the edge of being a

designer store and too fashion-forward for our line."

Sonia nodded along like the rest of us. "Exactly. So, maybe Sue Ellen is right about Dixie's presentation. Trendy and forward enough for Milgram's consumers, but too much for the more middle-of-the-road Bainbridge customer."

Hope blew the air out of her cheeks. "Sue Ellen knows who her customer is. She knows what she can sell and what she can't. If nothing else, Sue Ellen is a buyer who has a *cash register mentality*. Fashion-forward might make a gorgeous floor presentation...But let's face it, Bainbridge is in business to make money. If the floor setup doesn't ring the cash register, who cares if it looks beautiful?"

Queenie pursed her lips. "Maybe all well and good, but thanks to Sue Ellen and *the way* she attacked Dixie's abilities, Dixie is now *required* to present all projects to management for written approval before putting anything into work. Dixie is a seasoned professional who has been successfully doing her job description for almost a decade. She interpreted this management approval step normally required for a newbie, as a de facto demotion and a giant step back in her career."

Hope said, "If that's the way she took it, maybe it's best if she resigns and goes to another store."

Sonia shook her head. "Regrettably, like a wad of gum sticks to a shoe, a mark like that follows you forever."

Queenie said, "With all the buyouts and consolidations going on in the industry, jobs like hers are few and far between. She was born and raised in Orange County in one of those small beachside towns dotting the coast. She's a California girl through and through. I don't see her accepting a position in a mid-west or southern state-based store."

I rubbed my chin. "Dixie is beyond furious."

Hope grimaced. "From the sound of it, mad enough to spit nails."

Sonia mused aloud. "Mad enough to make Sue Ellen pay?"

Joan widened her eyes. "Maybe Dixie tried to do *exactly…?*"

Hope gasped, "Yet Dixie didn't succeed because…"

Joan snorted. "Because as usual, uncooperative Sue Ellen failed to get with the program and eat the poisoned jelly beans."

Queenie slammed the heel of her hand on the table. "*Enough!* Lemme tell you ladies something. I've known Dixie Chandler a helluva lot longer than I've known *any of you.* Dixie is a good person." Queenie pointed her index finger j'accuse style at each of the Yentas. "And the Dixie I know is no more capable of murdering anybody than one of us is."

I dragged my eyes over Queenie's beet-red-angry face with a look of pity. Dixie Chandler was Queenie's dear friend. And my words were going to sting. Didn't mean I shouldn't say them. Sometimes your closest friend is the one to force you to see the truth and not allow you to look away. I covered my hand over Queenie's and squeezed hers to soften the blow. "AJ Yakamura once said something I've never forgotten. '*You'd be surprised at the terrible things good people are capable of if they're pushed far enough.*' "

Chapter Twenty

Because I am a firm believer in the adage loose lips sink ships, I made blabby Hope pinky-swear she'd keep my going through Michael's desk and his garage strictly between us. Good gravy, if Queenie had a clue about my latest adventure, she'd birth a cow.

For security purposes, I spent a good portion of the night hunkered down in the houseboat galley transferring the photos I took of Michael's files from my phone to my tablet. Once the photos were transferred, I deleted them from my phone. If Heaven forbids, Michael found out I'd photographed his files and he managed to confiscate my phone, he'd find nothing except cute pictures of Siggie.

Michael's personal files were mildly informative. They focused on his day-to-day life and offered little else. Aside from being a gym rat who worked out daily, he was an avid tennis player and a few strokes above a duffer golfer. He played poker three times a week at a casino off the 710 freeway and was ahead more than behind. His two children attended a pricey private school in Brentwood. His wife was a realtor in Beverly Hills.

His financial files detailed an eye-popping net worth of fifty million dollars in cash, a slew of rental properties, and a fleet of race cars he inherited from his brother. He and his family lived mortgage-free in a five-bedroom

Spanish-style house on Camden Drive in Beverly Hills, featuring an Olympic-sized pool and tennis court in the half-acre-sized backyard. Michael maintained his partnership in the local delivery service but is not active daily. One thing was sure: No one had to throw a benefit for Michael Chennault.

Based on the files of the top twenty accounts which constituted seventy-five percent of the company's volume, Ditzy Swimwear suffered a serious profit decline since Michael bought it. Good thing Michael didn't depend on Ditzy Swimwear to support his family. If an income from Ditzy is how he fed his children, they would go hungry.

Ditzy suffered the biggest loss with Bainbridge Department Store. While the company *volume* was ahead twenty-two percent, Ditzy's *profits* dropped close to forty percent. It begged the question why? No change in designer or the fit of the garments, no huge retail markdown issues, and other than the loss of Bainbridge, Ditzy maintained a respectable account list. His cash sales? Astronomical. So why was the company awash in red ink? The last financial summary file was the telling of the tale. A second set of books. Michael was cooking the books and stealing his own company blind.

The file marked in red "*S.E. M.*" is the one that took my breath away. A spreadsheet detailing proposed monthly cash payments of $10,000.00 to Sue Ellen in exchange for a guaranteed 5% increase in full-price orders per month. Good grief! Thank the Goddess Sue Ellen is a straight shooter and refused the deal. If she accepted it, the Bainbridge swimwear department would be transformed into a Ditzy Swimwear store in a matter of months. If she took the bribe, how could she explain the volume decline of other more profitable vendors or ever justify all those orders to one supplier to her management? She couldn't. But even if by some miracle she managed to, if the Ditzy styles' sales tanked, Michael's position is he'd paid upfront and never give her a dime in markdown money. Her department profit margins would take a dive and tank below any possible redemption and she'd no doubt lose her job. Sue Ellen didn't take Michael's $10k monthly bribe, but she gave him a million reasons to destroy her. If I didn't find the Easter Bunny's real killer, Michael Chennault would succeed in ruining an innocent woman's life. Merde.

****

The next night was moonless and the perfect condition to snoop around in Michael's garage in the valley. The garage is located behind an abandoned warehouse on Saticoy Street in the old part of the industrial section of Van Nuys.

With no streetlights to guide me behind the abandoned warehouse, it took three tries around the block until I found the unmarked garage. Now, where the hell do I park? Tooling around town in a bubblegum pink vintage convertible is fun, but at times like this sticking out like a sore thumb could get me killed. I drove around the block again. Plenty of spots on the side streets…regrettably, all twenty-four-hour permit parking only. Just as well. I didn't relish hoofing it from the car parked two blocks away to the garage in such a rough neighborhood alone at night. Nevertheless, I needed to find a secluded spot.

Other than a bar featuring line dancing and blaring loud Country and Western music in the middle of the block on Saticoy, the area was completely deserted. Not a single light in a building, not a car or truck parked. Not exactly the safest place, however. I was running out of options, so I drove down the alley behind the bar. Even if I were willing to chance to leave my car behind the bar, it didn't matter. The parking lot was filled. Crap.

I checked the time. Ten-thirty. An involuntary shiver crawled down my spine as three tough-looking guys I hadn't noticed before passed a cigarette or a joint around on the street corner two doors down from the garage. The later it became, the more dangerous. My courage diminished with each tick of the clock.

I drove farther down the alley to behind the garage. The good news? Four unoccupied parking spots in front of the garage door. The bad news? I pulled into the middle one closest to the door and a motion-detector overhead light turned on and lit up the back of the garage like a beacon. My heart jumped to my throat as I prayed the motion detector wasn't equipped with a silent alarm. I pulled out of the parking space and when the light went off, thank the Goddess no cops in squad cars blaring their sirens raced around to the back of the garage.

The sides of the garage were wide enough to accommodate my car and deep enough to hide it. I pulled into the end of the narrow space on the left side. I killed the engine, pulled a flashlight and Hope's key out of my hobo bag, and climbed out of the car. I opened the trunk, took a black nylon car cover out, and threw it over the convertible.

I cleared the drainpipe and crept along the wall of the garage keeping my back flush up against the rough stucco. I turned left at the end of the building. Before I approached the garage door, I looked back to see if the outline of my car was visible. The moonless night helped the car cover blend my concealed convertible into the inky darkness.

I'd written the alarm security code on the palm of my hand. Mental head slap. Such a moron. My palms sweated and the numbers bled together and blurred. I squinted and held my palm perpendicular to the tip of my nose and angled the flashlight so it hit the numbers yet did not blind me.

I fished a pair of thin surgical gloves out of the hobo that I'd pilfered from Snip's office. Overly cautious? Not on your life. Distrusting Michael Chennault kept unsavory types of company, so he probably dusted for fingerprints twice a day. Of course, I'd never been in trouble with the law. Okay, let me clarify the statement. At least not to the level of having my fingerprints taken—yet. So, even if Michael had a snitch in one of the cop shops, my prints wouldn't be in the system.

I pointed the flashlight beam at the keypad and punched in the sequence of numbers. A half-dozen combinations later, three beeps and three flashes of a red light said the alarm was disarmed. I keyed open the padlock and the metal garage door slid open. I ran in and pushed a button and the garage door slid back down. I reset the alarm outside. Hopefully, the motion detector was only on the outside, or in around three minutes the place will be swarming with cop cars from the Panorama City precinct two blocks away. And unless I either found a fabulous hiding spot or had one helluva good story as to why I was sneaking around inside Michael Chennault's garage, I'd be on my way to the big house.

For a good ten minutes, I didn't dare move a muscle. I barely breathed as I pressed my ear against the garage door and strained to hear any sirens. Not a siren or screeching tires. The only sound? The jackhammer pounding of my heart thundering in my ears. I chanced a glance at my watch: eleven on the nose. I gave myself a twenty-minute limit to search the garage and find…no idea what, but I'd recognize it if I saw it. I waved the flashlight in an arc to get the lay of the land. From the outside, you couldn't gauge the actual size of the garage. Surprisingly, I eyeballed the rectangular-shaped interior at around three thousand square feet.

Three of the four interior corners of the room leading to the center were each occupied by a sleek, gleaming, low-to-the-ground Formula One race car. Each car rested on a set of wide racing tires. The empty fourth corner is where the racecar Michael entered in the weekend's race normally sat. The center of the room housed a hydraulic lift for mechanics to work on the cars.

The full length of the east wall supported a long metal workbench with drawers attached underneath it. Every conceivable tool and drill hung on the wall above it suspended by industrial-strength steel hooks. The west wall ran the length of the building and held three shelves filled with spare racing tires. An air hose attached to an air tank, an electronic tire pressure gauge, a hydraulic jack, and an electronic lug wrench plugged into a socket lined up like sentries next to the wall.

Since the driver barely had room to fit in the cab, and there was no glove box or a trunk to stash things, I left the vehicles for last. I opened every drawer and toolbox on the workbench and found nothing out of the ordinary. I crossed the room and stood on a ladder to search all three levels between and behind the tires. Nada. So far, this little adventure on the wild side? A colossal waste of time.

I walked the length of the garage and entered a neat-as-a-pin office at the back. Photos of Michael, his late brother, Louis, and pit crews working on race cars and celebrating victories decorated the walls. If any dirt is to be found, the odds are it will be in the office. If this room was cleansed of evidence, I was clean out of luck.

Two large closets facing one another stretched the length of the side walls. They buffeted a five-drawer metal desk sitting in the middle of the office. A heavy-looking steel combination safe sat under a window on the wall next to the left closet. I rifled through the closets only to find a wardrobe of racing jumpsuits, boots, and helmets in one and Michael's civilian wardrobe and shoes, and a collection of tennis rackets and golf clubs in the other one.

Next to a three-drawer file cabinet, a two-tiered credenza sat behind the desk and held numerous trophies and ribbons. The file cabinet drawers were stuffed to the gills with paid invoices separated by vendor and year, going back five years. I skipped the years Louis was alive and focused on the last two when Michael took over. There was not enough time to go through every invoice, so I photographed a dozen recently paid invoices fitting the timeframe of the murder. Hopefully, something incriminating wasn't hiding in plain sight I'd overlooked. I forced myself to push the unsettling thought out of my head and soldiered on.

A laser jet copier sat adjacent to the desk. A six-button phone and an adding machine sat stationed to the left side and a top-of-the-line computer was in the center of the desktop. I sat in an oversized leather chair soft as a pat of butter behind the desk and sunk up to my neck. I wriggled and squirmed and grabbed the armrest to propel myself forward. I bent over and yanked on the handle of the middle drawer. The drawer held two packs of gum, another half-empty box of condoms, and a pair of aviator-style sunglasses housed in a hardshell case as well as an assortment of pens, pencils, paper clips, and scratch paper. The only thing missing? A smoking gun.

The lower left-side drawer held a series of hanging folders holding open invoices and two books of blank order forms. The top left-side drawer housed a small tape recorder, an expensive-looking video camera, and an electronic tablet. I hit the play button on the tape recorder and smiled as I listened to presumably Michael's children singing an off-key rendition of Happy Birthday to their dad. I tried opening the tablet but like the computer, it was password protected. I tapped a half-dozen guesses and gave up after wasting five precious minutes.

The top right-side drawer housed an assortment of catalogs for car parts, paints, and emergency kits, as well as books on repairing or maintaining engines, and a thick address book containing supplier names and contact information.

So far, every inch of the space I'd searched said this was a legitimate business. I scratched the crown of my head. I am a professional sales exec. I make my living sizing people up. Is it possible to have misread this guy so badly? Was he merely a bully and nothing more sinister?

One last drawer. If it held nothing incriminating, then time to admit I'd climbed up the wrong tree, lock the joint up tight, and boogie. I tugged on the lower right-side drawer handle, but it didn't budge. I bent over and discovered a locked drawer. I opened the middle one to look for the key. I twisted my torso around like a pretzel, turned my head to be perpendicular to the drawer, and beamed my flashlight up. I crossed my mental fingers that Michael taped the key to the top of the drawer. Naturally, no such luck.

Think, think. What would MacGyver do now? I pulled a metal nail file from my manicure kit in the hobo. Unfortunately, the tip was too thick and wouldn't go in far enough to jimmy the lock. I scrounged around the desktop and took a silver letter opener out of a mesh office supply container. The tip was thin enough, but too short to reach the lock tumblers. I straightened a paperclip and jiggled the tumblers using its tip, but nothing clicked. My heart sank.

If the contents of the drawer were important enough to keep it locked, it stood to reason Michael took the key. A stab of defeat pierced my heart. As I stood to leave, my gut screamed, "Wait a damned Cincinnati minute! It doesn't mean an extra copy isn't in the office."

I checked my watch. Crap. Maybe twelve minutes, no more, to find the key, open the drawer, and examine the contents. No time for a full search. I turned a visual one-eighty around the room. The most logical hiding place? Think, think. I opened the middle drawer again and pulled it all the way out. I shoved my arm in and felt something way in the back of the drawer. I emptied everything in the drawer onto the desk. A plastic tampon case fell out and bounced diagonally across the blotter. Huh? I'd run out of plausible places to search, so for giggles and squeaks, I opened the case. The only item inside was an oddly folded hundred-dollar bill and a small gold key with no markings wrapped inside the C-note. One short flick of the wrist and a quick turn to the right and Bingo. Bongo. Jackpot. We have a winner, ladies and gentlemen.

A dozen dog-eared ledgers were packed tight in the drawer. I pulled them all out and stacked them on the desk. They were organized by year, the earliest ones on the bottom and the most recent ones on the top. I returned the older ones to the desk drawer, careful to put them back in the correct yearly order.

I flipped through the first ledger. Michael bought into an auto racetrack consortium the year prior. He now owned a controlling interest in three racetracks around the country and made a killing the second year. Seemed like a helluva conflict of interest, yet apparently not illegal.

Ledger number two detailed the profits and losses of his racecar business. Michael was in the red on one car and making a fortune off the other three. Fingers of disappointment squeezed my heart. So far, these ledgers were a big fat nothing burger.

Time check. Seven minutes. I put ledger three back in the drawer and hesitated to close it. I debated whether to go through the last ledger or ditch it. Based on everything else I'd examined, I doubted I'd find anything helpful, yet curiosity propelled my fingers to take it out.

The columns detailed the profits and losses of MMC Pharmaceuticals. Holy guacamole! Michael Maurice Chennault was a drug dealer who specialized in boutique drugs. The ledger pages were organized alphabetically by drug, and if I read the numbers correctly, page number two told me everything I needed to know. *Botox* was his number one volume drug. Ding, ding. We've got a winner, ladies and gentlemen. I fired up the phone camera app and shot photos of every page of the ledger.

To be on the safe side, I e-mailed them to myself to my personal e-mail address and then deleted the photos from my phone.

Chapter Twenty-One

As I finished returning the last of the ledgers back into the drawer, the quiet-as-a-tomb-silence of the building shattered when the garage door slowly creaked open.

I turned the face of the flashlight downward and shoved it between my legs. I leaned over to the light to wrap the key back into the C-note and return it to the case. Then I shoved it into the back left corner of the desk. I swept everything else into the drawer helter-skelter with a flick of a wrist and winced as the items rattled loudly and bounced around back into the drawer. I prayed whoever opened the door wasn't inside the garage yet.

The answer to the question came by the count of two Mississippi's later. The voices of two tough-sounding men echoed through the front of the cavernous room and my heart leaped to my throat.

A gravelly voice that sounded like it needed clearing spat, "Holy crap! Man, that punk Ricky is toast! The boss is gonna go ape-shit when he finds out Ricky forgot to lock the garage door!"

Did the voice sound vaguely familiar or was it merely wishful thinking? I wracked my memory to match it to a name and drew a big honkin' blank.

A raspy kind of voice usually associated with a four-pack-a-day cigarette smoker replied, "No shit. Even if the alarm is set, it wouldn't take an experienced break-and-enter team to clean the place out before the cops arrived."

Mr. Gravelly said, "Looks like nothing is missing. All the cars and equipment are in the right place."

Mr. Raspy laughed evilly. "Lucky Ricky. Maybe the boss will just cut the punk's nuts off and not kill him."

Mr. Gravelly said, "Grab the equipment on the list Michael said Ricky forgot to bring. Then stow everything in the bed of the truck. Take the tarp out of the toolbox and cover the truck bed. Be sure to anchor the tarp down using the eye hooks so it doesn't blow off once we get on the freeway."

I bit my lip. I know that gravelly voice. Think. Think. For crying out loud, your life depends on it! Zippo. Despite my best efforts to match a name to the voice, I drew a blank.

Mr. Raspy asked, "Okay, but what are *you* doing while I'm bustin' my hump? The list is as long as my arm. It'll go a lot faster if we divide it up. We've got a long drive ahead of us, so whaddya say?"

Mr. Gravelly clucked his tongue. "I'm lettin' ya off easy."

Mr. Raspy laughed. "BS. In which man's army are you lettin' me off easy?"

Mr. Gravelly tsked. "Trust me. You got the better end of the deal. While you're packing the truck, I'm going into the office and calling the boss. That's gonna be a fun conversation. Not."

Holy guacamole. I killed the flashlight and looked around for the best place to hide.

Mr. Raspy said, "Better you than me, pal. Hopefully,

Michael doesn't kill the messenger."

Mr. Gravelly said, "Take a whiff will ya? Is my sniffer off or do you smell *ladies' perfume*?"

Mr. Raspy inhaled a snortful of air through his honker. "Damn, you're right." His laugh was like sandpaper scratching against wood. "Maybe Ricky brought a broad with him and he got lucky. Horny bastard probably hadn't been laid in a while and got so excited, he forgot to lock up."

I sniffed the air and then held my forearm up to my nose. Christ on a crutch, he was right. Regrettably, the perfume infused in the room belonged to me, not Ricky's girlfriend.

Mr. Gravelly said, "Nah. Ricky was here early in the morning. The scent is way too strong. Whoever was in the joint, it wasn't too long ago. The lock wasn't broken, so whoever it was had a key. Why she'd be nosing around, I dunno, but my money says it's the boss' old lady."

I opened the closet door on the left and cringed as it squeaked. There was too much crap inside for me to push everything aside and not make any noise.

Mr. Raspy replied. "You ever seen her? A fancy broad like her? Not a chance in hell she'd risk breakin' one of her fingernails. Mebbe we should search the place. Mebbe Ricky's bimbo is still around? I wouldn't put it past numb nut Ricky to lock the broad up after he screwed her."

I closed the closet door on the left and looked under the desk. Unfortunately, the desk style featured an open front. Mental head slap. Mr. Gravelly will sit behind the desk when he calls Michael. Even if Mr. Gravelly didn't spy me on his way into the office, I'm small, but if he stretched his legs out under the desk… A cold rivulet of sweat crept down my spine. I shuddered at the price I'd pay when Michael found out.

Mr. Gravelly spat. "Come on, that's just plain stupid. Don't ya think she'd come out and be thrilled to be rescued?"

"Yeah, I guess you're right. Okay, go make the call and I'll get the gear settled into the truck. By the time Michael gets done screaming his lungs out, I'll be ready to roll." He laughed. "Watch out. Mebbe Ricky told the broad he'd be back. Maybe the bimbo didn't check if the door was open and she's sitting at the desk waiting for him."

Mr. Gravelly clucked his tongue. "There's a phone on the desk. Even a bimbo knows how to dial one…"

I scrambled into the closet on the right and pushed my way into the back corner. I scrunched my body into as small a ball as possible and covered myself with a bunch of nylon racing jumpsuits. Mr. Gravelly turned on the office light and pulled the chair out from behind the desk. From the way the chair springs loudly complained, Mr. Gravelly must be a big man. Cripes, I am so screwed.

Mr. Gravelly gulped a big mouthful of air and greeted Michael. "Yeah, boss. It's me, Tony. Listen, everything's cool, but we've got a little situation…"

Tony, Tony…didn't I meet a new hire at Ditzy named Tony the last day I worked at the company? Think, think. I wracked my poor addled brain. Maybe yes…or maybe I'm just going crazy. Toss a coin.

I felt around in my jeans pocket for my phone. For once I remembered to turn off the power. My luck, some yahoo ordering a late-night takeout pizza from a twenty-four-hour-delivery joint misdials and gets my number.

And then? May I take your order, please? Not.

I leaned as far as possible toward the front of the closet without tipping over and turned my head to eavesdrop on Tony's "*conversation*" with Michael. No need to strain my ears. Michael yelled so loud I heard him through the thick closet doors swearing like a drunk sailor. I prayed Mr. Gravelly was too preoccupied trying to calm Michael down that it never occurred to him to check the closets since my perfume still permeated the office.

Chapter Twenty-Two

Bleary-eyed, I dragged my weary bones to the mart the next morning and served the Yentas their coffees. Joan gave me the once-over as I handed her a steaming mug. I grimaced as I gingerly eased my tush into the seat.

Joan asked, "So, who won the fight and does the other guy look as bad as you?"

My powers of control were too weak to dare look across the table at Hope for help, so I kept my peepers peeled to the inside of my coffee cup. My addled brain was a bit scrambled from barely surviving the festivities of the prior evening. I took a big glug of coffee to buy some time to devise an answer that wouldn't lead to more probing questions I didn't care to respond to. Nothing brilliant came to mind, so I smiled wanly and punted. "Har-har Miss Smarty Pants. Aren't you the clever one so early, and without a jolt of java, no less?"

No fool, our Joan. Even caffeine-free, she can sniff out a dodge with the best of them. She eyed me over the rim of her glasses in an annoying kindergarten teacher look of disapproval she's honed over the years into an art form. She impatiently tapped the rim of her mug with a teaspoon. "Be that as it may…so, what's the story, morning glory? Why do you look like a bus ran you over?"

If she only knew.

Queenie grinned evilly and toasted me with her mug. "She's got two drop-dead gorgeous men chasing her tush all over town now and competing for her attention. Maybe she's burning the candle from both ends?"

Good grief. As if my life isn't complicated enough, now she adds *the two of them* to the equation. All the same, never one to look a gift horse in the mouth, I grabbed the life preserver she'd inadvertently tossed me and saved myself from a whole lotta aggravation I couldn't face right then. Eventually, I'd fess up... maybe. Trust me, it's gonna take a helluva lot more coffee and gumption than I had either of them at the moment.

I blushed from the neck up to my scalp, hopefully concealing my so-called lying face. I grinned as I lied through my teeth. "Let's just say never go out on a school night if your homework isn't done because you'll have to do it *the next morning* or pay the penalty..."

A chorus of catcalls and wolf whistles ensued and I responded in kind with a universally distributed middle finger salute. Mercifully, my sly insinuation of a lust fest satisfied their curiosity and we continued our coffee klatch discussing mundane subjects designed to keep me out of hot water with my colleagues. On our way out of the coffee shop, Hope tugged my shirtsleeve and tipped her head toward Shoots N' Blooms, the mart flower shop. I gave her an odd look but followed her lead. "I love your taste in fresh flowers. Help me pick out a bouquet to send to my sister for her birthday."

Hope and I waved good-bye to our colleagues as they squeezed into a crowded elevator. Once the elevator door closed, I turned to Hope and arched a brow. "*You love my taste in fresh flowers?* Good grief, woman... *That's* the best story you're able to concoct?"

She shrugged. "Shoot me. I don't think fast on my feet. It's the first thing that came to mind." She pointed to the flower shop and laughed. "As it turns out, I do need to send my sister a birthday bouquet." Hope smiled sardonically. "I just don't need any help picking out the flowers."

I motioned her toward the mart entrance on Main Street. "Let's take a walk. Too many big ears in the mart."

She nodded her understanding and we headed toward Bainbridge Department Store. We walked in companionable silence until we crossed Ninth Street and headed west. We crossed onto Broadway and passed Bainbridge's south entrance and the smile died on Hope's beautiful heart-shaped face. "Thanks to you, I got only a few minutes of sleep last night." She cracked a yawn so wide it cut her face in half. "You had me up almost *all night* pacing the floor waiting for your phone call. I almost split my spleen from worry. I broke down and called your cell phone...*three times* and left you messages to call me. When you didn't answer or call back, just imagine all the horrible scenarios going through my mind. By dawn I was frantic. I thought the worst. Michael returns unexpectedly, catching you inside the garage, killing you, and burying your body in some Godforsaken field in the middle of nowhere. Why the hell didn't you call me like you promised to?"

I sighed. "I'm sorry I worried you. I didn't mean to...it's a long story. You sure you want to hear it all now?"

She smiled grimly. "Unlike a fine wine, age won't

improve this kind of story." Hope checked her watch and pulled the cell phone out of her purse. "Buster should be in the showroom by now. Lemme call him and say I'm gonna be late." Hope made her excuses to Buster and ended the call. She pointed to Auntie Bea's, a greasy spoon diner at the end of the block. "Until I saw you alive and kicking this morning, the concept of food made me ill. I don't know about you, but I'm famished. A stack of Bea's blueberry pancakes sounds mighty appealing. Whaddya say?"

****

Hope's eyes widened almost as big as the saucer holding her coffee cup. As though I was reading her a bedtime story, she listened intently with no interruptions or questions as I detailed the events of the previous night. I finished telling the tale and I swear Michael's key burned my palm as I took it out of the hobo and handed it back to Hope.

"A helluva story. However, you left out one important part..." She swallowed a glug of coffee and twisted her lips into a wicked smile. "If those two gumbahs locked the garage from the outside, how did you get out?"

I grinned like a Cheshire cat. "I saved the best part of the story for last. Once they left, I turned off the alarm from the inside and tried to open the door. Naturally, it wouldn't budge. Dawn would break in only a few short hours. I had to get out and pronto before the sun came up while the area was still deserted. All I needed was some nosy early riser to see me sneaking out of the garage and call the cops. The fastest way out? Pushing the door open using one of the racecars. I checked each one to see if the keys were in the ignition. Of course, no such luck. I

137

searched everywhere, but no keys. I even tried a bunch of combinations of numbers on the safe, but it proved trickier than finding a needle in a haystack. Since none of them worked, I went to plan B."

I laughed. "It's a good thing I'm a devoted MacGyver fan and not afraid of heights. I found a tow rope in one of the drawers in the garage. I tied a loose sailor's knot at the end. I climbed onto the top of the safe against the wall while holding the rope. I stood on my tiptoes and lassoed the handle on the window by looping it sideways and pulling the knot closed. I anchored the hobo strap diagonally across my boobs and hoisted myself up the rope to the window. Thank the Goddess the window didn't stick and it pushed open going outward. And it's a damned good thing I'm thin and short or I'd have been shit outta luck. I pulled the rope up and swung my legs over the window ledge to the drainpipe. I dropped the rope out the window and wrapped my legs around the drainpipe. I grabbed the drainpipe using my left hand, unhooked the rope off the handle with my right, and let it drop to the ground. I rappelled my way down the drainpipe like a mountain climber."

I grimaced and rubbed my back. "I lost my footing a couple of times and bounced off the building. I scraped my back on the rough stucco surface. I ruined a brand-new sweater and it hurts like a bitch when I bend over. I hit the ground, grabbed the rope, ran to the front, and unlocked the garage. I went inside the office, climbed on the safe, looped the rope around the window handle, and pulled the window shut. I jerked the rope loose, climbed down, and returned the tow rope to the drawer. I locked the garage door, reset the alarm, tore the tarp off the convertible, and boogied a few minutes before dawn broke."

Hope pursed her lips. "You almost got yourself killed getting the goods on Michael. Exactly how are you gonna use the information?"

I grinned. "No idea. Stay tuned for further developments."

Chapter Twenty-Three

I prayed it wasn't an omen when Saturday dawned foggy and overcast as Siggie and I hit the streets for our morning constitutional. By the time we left A Jolt of Java, the sun pushed its way through the gun-metal gray clouds shrouding the Washington Street pier. I bought two biggie cups of high-test coffee-one for me and one for Pop, the senior citizen fisherman I'd befriended several years ago who cast his line from the same spot on the pier for over a decade.

I took a restorative sip of coffee as we headed for the pier. "So, Siggie, did I do the right thing by accepting Miguel's party invitation? Or do you think I'm leading him on? I mean, it's just a party, right? No biggie."

Who was I trying to convince? Me or my dog?

Siggie turned his big head to the side and gifted me with one of his practiced *good grief* looks.

I clucked my tongue. "Okay, you're giving me the look." *Mr. Who Me?* blinked guilelessly. My four-legged friend innocent? Ha. My Aunt Fannie's tush. "Cut out the crap. You do so know the look. The one says you're a little late asking the question. You're right…tonight is the big event so no chickening out now. Besides, I spent a bucket of bucks on a dress, matching shoes, and a purse who knows if I'll ever wear them again?"

Honest to Goddess, my wisenheimer hound rolled

his eyes. A nasty habit he picked up from Queenie…certainly not from me…

"You should be thrilled. You're spending the day at Muriel's. Since I've no idea how late I'll be coming home, you'll be bunking on her boat tonight."

Siggie smiled and barked two short woofs of joyous anticipation. No fool my pooch. Muriel had a big day planned and will spoil him silly. For starters, a romp at the dog park, followed by an hour-long cruise down to the Redondo Beach Marina for a playday at Muriel's friend Sadie and her golden retriever Maxie Boy's boat. Then he'd top off the day eating a special evening meal of gourmet dog food from the Woof and Barkery. Truth be told, I was kind of jealous.

We spent a half-hour visiting Pop and then headed back to the marina. I dropped Sigmund and all his gear off at Muriel's and went back to the houseboat to pack my ensemble and makeup in a garment bag. I locked up the houseboat and walked around Palawan Way to Admiralty and turned south to the Marina del Rey Beach Club, a quarter down the street and diagonally across the channel from my houseboat.

I met Queenie at Le Bagel Bar Du Jour inside the club lobby. We took our food to the outside patio overlooking the channel. We slathered thick schmears of cream cheese all over our bagels and gobbled them like we hadn't eaten in a month of Sundays. Strong cups of coffee completed the tasty treat.

Queenie tapped her index finger on the tip of her nose. "I'm curious. You had your knickers tied in a sailor's knot over the way your relationship with Miguel might change by your attending this shindig. So, what made you decide to accept his invitation?"

"My mother."

"*Your mother?*"

"Yeah, my mother. I told her my fears and she accused me of overreacting." I rolled my eyes. "Overreacting my ass. All my mother's friend's daughters are married and making them grandmas. My mother is so anxious for me to get married and settle down, she practically jumped through the phone when I told her about the party."

Queenie slapped her palm on the table, making a sound like a cracked whip. "Lemme get this straight. You're reticent over going to the party because you think it signals you're ready to make a commitment to Miguel. So, you call your mother for advice...a mother *you know* wants you married...and after talking to her, you decide to go to the party. Right?"

"Yeah, in a nutshell, you hit the nail on the head."

Queenie huffed, "You don't need a friend. You need a psychiatrist."

"Your support is overwhelming."

"I live to serve."

Queenie snapped her fingers. "If you're having a change of heart, bail out. We're at the beach. Maybe a sudden attack of bad clams?"

"Tempting, but I won't do that to Miguel or his family."

Queenie clucked her tongue. "Too bad you have a conscience."

"Yeah, too bad. I'd make a terrible buyer."

"Ain't it the truth, sister...ain't it the truth?"

Queenie gave me an expectant look. "So, what's the story with this party?"

"Fifteen is a special birthday for girls in the Hispanic

culture and they celebrate with a type of coming-of-age party. The best way to describe it? Miguel said it's sort of a cotillion and a Bar Mitzvah party mixed together, if you squint. The celebration is called a Quinceanera or the fiesta de Quinceanera, quince años, fiesta de quince años, and quinces. It is a celebration of a girl's fifteenth birthday. It has pre-Columbian roots in Mexico from the Aztecs and is widely celebrated by girls throughout Hispanic America. It is a huge event and a highlight for both the birthday girl and the whole family. Before the party a special Mass is celebrated at the church called Misa de Accion de Gracias, which means a Thanksgiving Mass. After the Mass, then the guests go to a venue specializing in Quinceanera events and the party begins."

I grinned. "Think a sweet sixteen party spiced by salsa. The party has some interesting elements. Central to the celebration is traditional Mexican food for friends and family. After the meal, fifteen pinatas are filled to break open and the birthday cake has the number fifteen on it. As she blows out the fifteen candles on the cake, the birthday girl is serenaded by the guests who sing Las Mananitas, which means the tomorrows. Miguel said it's a traditional Hispanic happy birthday song. The birthday girl receives a special gift—La Ultima Muneca—the last doll—to signify going forward she will no longer be a little girl and signals she is now considered a young woman. These include all the Quinceanera traditions—the Court of Honor made up of her closest friends, a religious ceremony prior to the party, a first waltz at the reception. The birthday girl wears her first formal style dress and a tiara signed by the number fifteen on the crown. She exchanges her flat shoes for high heels, receives her first ramo de flores—her first bouquet of flowers, and male dance partners called Chambelanes dance with her to the music of a Mariachi band."

Queenie pursed her lips. "This gig is kinda out of your lane. Do you know the appropriate dress style?"

I shook my head. "No. I said the same thing to Miguel. His older sister, Adela called me after I accepted Miguel's invitation. Adela is the birthday girl—Isabella's mother. Adela invited me to lunch and go shopping for a dress afterwards. We met at The Blue China Moon Café last Saturday for Moo-Shoo. After we ate, I suggested we go to the new section of jobbers who specialize in dressy clothes on Los Angeles Street east of the mart."

Queenie reminded me of my nana as she tapped her fingertip on her nose. "Is his sister nice? Is she like Miguel?"

"She is delightfully charming. Smart as a whip and like him, fast on her feet. Plus, she has a wicked sense of humor…she did an imitation of Miguel on his high horse and I almost wet my panties." I fingered the garment bag. "It's a good thing Adela took me shopping or I'd have picked way too fancy a dress. The guests are not expected to outshine the birthday girl. So, Adela steered me towards classy street-length dresses in more neutral colors. We found a wonderful shop called Elegance on a side street that had a huge selection of dresses in my size."

Queenie pointed to the garment bag lying across a chair next to me. "So, tell me about your outfit."

"It's a gorgeous beige raw silk sheath street-length dress with three-quarter length sleeves and a Mandarin collar. Next, we went over to Bainbridge's and found the perfect shoes—dyed to match silk beige pumps—two-inch heels with a beige fleur d'lis attached to the top of each shoe. High enough to make a fashion statement and low enough so I can dance and not fall on my ass. I have a beige beaded evening bag and my nana's beige mesh knit shawl that has mother of pearl beads, shell appliques, and lace embellishments as my wrap."

"The embellishment style of your nana's shawl sounds a lot like my fashion school senior project sweater." My heart ached as Queenie's eyes filled. "It's a damned shame Diane stole it out of my office and used it to frame me for Butch Oldham's murder. The style would have been a perfect match for your outfit tonight. I've tried everything. Unfortunately, nothing gets the bloodstains out."

****

Late afternoon, I squirmed impatiently in a seat facing Queenie's vanity mirror. Queenie clamped her fingers tightly around my right shoulder and growled. "Hold still or I'm gonna spill this fairy dust all over you!"

I arranged to get ready for the party and have Miguel pick me up at Queenie's house. A houseboat is a cool place to live. Regrettably, it's not the right place to jump off wearing fancy-schmancy digs and high heels. I am deathly allergic to her two pampered cats, so Queenie put Sampson and Delilah in the garage for the afternoon.

I sighed. "I don't know why I let you and Eddy in the beauty shop convince me to put that crap in my hair." I clucked my tongue. "Maybe we shouldn't do it. I'm not supposed to outshine the birthday girl."

Queenie snorted. "For crying out loud, it's not like you're gonna waltz into the party wearing a diamond tiara. A few sprinkles of fairy dust will just give some highlights to your brown hair."

Truly not a battle worth fighting. "Fine. Sprinkle a little, just don't overdo it. Fairy dust isn't exactly my style."

Queenie finished her fussing and held a hand mirror behind my head to see the complete finished product. Holy guacamole. My hair gleamed positively lustrous.

She checked her watch and pointed to the vanity. "Okay. Chop-chop, fairy princess. Better hustle your bustle. You've got just enough time to put the last touches on your makeup and get dressed. Prince Charming is due in twenty minutes and since he's never late, we don't want to keep him waiting."

The doorbell rang as I walked down the stairs from Queenie's bedroom to the living room. Queenie turned for a last-minute inspection and her eyes popped. "Oh my Goddess, you're absolutely gorgeous." She patted her cheeks and kvelled like a proud mama. "Good gravy! After Miguel gets a gander at you so smokin' hot, you'll set the party venue on fire, he'll never let go of you. Don't be surprised if he proposes by the end of the evening."

Crap on a crumpet.

Just what I needed…no pressure…right?

Damn the freakin' fairy dust.

Chapter Twenty-Four

Suspended twinkling lights entwined through magnificent arrangements of lush tropical flowers transformed the elegantly decorated ballroom of El Palacio Royal on Sunset Blvd. into an enchanted fairyland fit for a princess.

Thirty round tables, each set for six guests and featuring crystal vase centerpieces filled with multicolored baby roses, were assembled in a semi-circle that faced the Mariachi band stand. The head table for the birthday girl, her parents and grandparents sat stationed in the center of the semi-circle. Miguel led me to the head table and introduced me to his parents, sisters and brothers, and of course, to the birthday girl. Miguel's mother, sisters, and Isabella all fawned over me as though I was the guest of honor. Oh boy. We took our seats at the table adjacent to the head table. I blushed from head to toe as I caught Miguel staring at me.

After a dinner menu of traditional Mexican cuisine, the lights dimmed at precisely eight and the Mariachi band struck up Las Mananitas. All the guests stood to applaud as the birthday girl, wearing an exquisite pale pink floor-length off-the-shoulder organza gown and a sparkling tiara emblazoned with the number fifteen on it nestled in the crown of her wavy black hair, was escorted into the room by her parents, grandparents, and the court of honor consisting of Isabella's six closest friends. Then the lights dimmed again, and the elaborate birthday cake ceremony took place. The Mariachi band played and an utterly radiant Isabella danced her first waltz.

Mid-way through the evening, Miguel and I made our way around the tables and chatted up all the other guests. We stopped at the fourth table and Miguel introduced me to Daniel Oliva and his wife Estella. Daniel is one of Miguel's high school friends, and the father of Isabella's closest friend, Elena. Daniel and Miguel went through the police academy together and Daniel is the Homicide-Robbery division Captain at the Panorama City precinct in the San Fernando Valley.

Once we made the rounds and the band started playing a lively number, Miguel smiled sardonically and pointed to our empty table. "Do you mind if we sit the next few out? My feet are killing me." He laughed. "I haven't been on my feet this much since my rookie days as a beat cop on Hollywood Blvd."

I pointed to my shoes and grinned. "No worries. Breaking in new shoes by a night of dancing isn't exactly a brain surgeon move."

Miguel waved in Daniel's direction. "It's such a coincidence Danny and I both ended up as Captains in our precincts. Yesterday we both attended the quarterly Captains conference at LAPD headquarters. We grabbed a beer and a burger after the meeting and swapped war stories. He told me about one of the oddest cases. His robbery team responded to a call about a break-in a couple of nights ago."

I widened my eyes. "Geesh, a break-in. Awful." Miguel studied my face as if I were a new species.

My blood ran cold as he explained. "Normally a call

regarding a break-in goes to the burglary division. This particular one came from the owner of a garage in the old industrial section of Van Nuys behind Saticoy Street housing his quartet of Formula One racecars. I'm pretty sure you know the victim. He's a competitor of yours. Michael Chennault—the guy who owns Ditzy Swimwear."

The flush of guilt crept up my neck as I willed my voice not to quaver. "Of course, I know him. My friend Hope works for him and she didn't say a word." I shrugged. "We don't know one another well, but Michael seems like a private kind of guy. Maybe he didn't tell her about the incident or if he did, he told her to keep it to herself."

"Mr. Chennault was out of town in Central California when the break-in occurred—at a racetrack preparing one of his Formula One cars for a weekend event. A number of critically-needed tools were inadvertently left in the garage by a pit crewman. Mr. Chennault contacted two of his employees to go to the garage, collect the tools, and drive them up north."

"Didn't the garage have an alarm?"

"Of course, it had an alarm, and this is why the story is so odd. When the two men arrived at the garage, they found the lock open, yet the alarm was armed, but nothing was missing."

I shrugged, "Seems as if whoever took the racecar up north armed the alarm and forgot to engage the lock."

Miguel shook his head. "The detectives interviewed the guy and at Mr. Chennault's insistence, Danny's team gave him a lie-detector test, which he passed with flying colors."

"Well, then somebody else who had access was at

the garage and failed to lock up. Any idea the number of people who have access to the garage?"

"Six. Mr. Chennault, his wife, three members of his pit crew, and your friend Hope."

My eyes bugged. "*Hope*? Why in the world does *she* need access to a garage housing Formula One cars?"

Miguel bunched his shoulders. "No idea. Maybe Chennault wanted someone local to have access if the rest of them were all out of town and there was an emergency."

"Maybe his wife was at the garage for some reason."

"Nope. Mrs. Chennault accompanied her husband up north. The oddest part of all of this is after the two men stepped into the garage, they both smelled ladies' perfume in the place."

"Obviously, Michael's wife went with him in the garage when they took the racecar out to go up north."

Miguel shook his head. "Uh-uh. Mr. and Mrs. Chennault left the night before. The pit crew prepped the car and flat-bedded it up to the racetrack. This leaves only one person left who had access to the garage—your friend Hope. Any idea why she would go inside the garage?"

"Not a clue unless Michael asked her to."

Miguel pursed his lips. "Or maybe a nameless nosy parker directed her to look around in the garage searching for…?"

Hmm. Not a bad guess, Mickey. Maybe that was why he was the chief of detectives. Nonetheless, he'd pissed me off big time. Just as I opened my mouth to make a righteously indignant, and likely relationship-ending comeback, Miguel's father appeared out of thin air and asked me to dance. I didn't want to make a scene and spoil Isabella's big night, so as appealing as it was, throttling Miguel in the middle of the celebration was out of the question. I spent the rest of the evening dancing with virtually every able-bodied man at the party and left Miguel alone to cool his heels.

The party certainly wasn't the appropriate place to duke this out once and for all, yet ignoring the elephant in the room much longer wasn't an option. By mutual silent consent, we agreed to put the argument if not behind us, at least to the side for the rest of the night. By the time the party ended, our better angels prevailed and we both took a step back from the cliff of relationship-ending oblivion.

Chapter Twenty-Five

Miguel pulled the SUV into his garage around twelve-thirty in the morning. We entered the back door into his bungalow-style two-bedroom house located in the flats of Brentwood. We walked through the open-style floor plan into the master bedroom.

Just as he folded me into his arms and kissed me with an intensity that curled my toes and sent a sizzling electric current to spark *every* single one of my nerve endings, six beeps signaling waiting messages bleeped from my cell phone. I went positively weak in the knees as Miguel slowly traced feathery kisses up my neck and nibbled my earlobe. He breathlessly mumbled, "Let it wait until tomorrow. It's probably your friend Queenie wanting the lowdown on the party."

Queenie might be anxious to get all the dirt on the party…but six messages this late at night? No way. No good news ever arrives in the middle of the night. My parents and siblings all lived at the other end of the country. My heart leapt to my throat. Please Goddess, please don't let it be one of them.

To Miguel's utter consternation, I wriggled out of his embrace. I glanced at the messages and my blood ran cold. All six were from Muriel Lobowsky. Oh. My. God. Siggie. Something happened to my dog! I hit the play button on the first message and my knees buckled.

"Holly, I'm so sorry to bother you at the party, but we've got a problem. Siggie is sick and I've taken him to the emergency pet hospital on Lincoln Blvd just north of Washington. The vet is examining him now. They haven't identified the problem yet. Please call me back as soon as you get this message. Hopefully, by then, I'll know more."

I stupidly didn't play the other five messages. My hand shook so badly as I tried to press the redial option, I missed it twice and hit my contacts list instead. I finally managed to press the right button and put the phone on speaker so Miguel could hear the conversation too.

Muriel picked up on the first ring.

My voice cracked as I choked out the question. "Muriel, is…he-he de-dead?"

Crusty old Muriel made no effort to mask her annoyance as she tsked a loud cluck of her tongue. *"Obviously,* you didn't *bother* to play the other five messages…"

Since she didn't burst into tears at the question and instead drilled me with one of her infamous sassy comments, apparently Siggie was still amongst the living. Thank the Goddess.

Duly chastened, I replied in a rare tone of contriteness. "You're right. I didn't. I apologize."

I glanced at my watch. Twelve-forty-five. "Are you back on your boat?"

"Nope, I'm still at the emergency hospital. I wouldn't leave until our boy was released and going home."

I gulped. "Good grief, it must be pretty serious for him to still be at the hospital."

Muriel sighed. "It is serious, but it could have been

a lot worse. I've no idea how he got a hold of it, but according to the Vet, Siggie ate a goodly amount of chocolate and suffered a nasty reaction."

I screeched loud as a barn owl. "*Chocolate!* How the hell did he get chocolate?" Exhaustion and fear failed to keep the j'accuse tone out of my voice. "*I* don't keep any on the boat now that *I* have a dog."

Muriel's normally gruff voice rose half a dozen octaves as she huffed in a tone of self-righteous indignation. "*Well, don't look at me. I know better and don't keep any on my boat either.*"

Guilt squeezed my heart. Muriel loves my dog almost as much as me. "Muriel, for crying out loud, calm your jets. I wasn't suggesting *you gave* it to him."

Fingers of irrational annoyance twisted my innards as Miguel's bushy eyebrows shot up to his forehead. He beamed a "*it sure sounded that way to me*" glance in my direction. What is that famous quote of Julius Caesar's? Oh, yeah. *We mock what we are to be.* As you're lithe to often lecture me, Mickey…mind your own beeswax.

Fortunately, Muriel chose not to call me out on it and sighed. "Whatever way he got it, he ate enough to give himself one helluva case of chocolate intoxication."

"No sense trying to figure this out over the phone." I squeaked a nervous giggle and peeked at Miguel. "We're in Brentwood. We'll be there in forty-five minutes."

****

Miguel's SUV hadn't pulled completely into the visitor's parking space when I jumped out and sprinted to a corrugated steel Quonset hut decorated by a colorful mural of Noah's Ark—replete with animals paired two by two—painted horizontally across the torso of the building. A life-size cutout of a Doctor Dolittle-like graphic character stood adjacent to the entrance and pointed to a sign painted in brightly-colored, slanted letters above the front door: "*Welcome creatures big and small to the Marina del Rey Emergency Animal Clinic.*"

I stepped into the empty waiting room and approached a middle-aged woman seated behind a knotty pine reception counter. She wore pink polyester scrubs stretched tightly across her ample bust. Her scrubs had the same Noah's Ark pattern as the one adorned on the outside of the building. The woman looked over tortoise-shell half-glasses readers perched precariously on the tip of her ski-jump nose. The corkscrew curls of her platinum blonde dyed hair briefly curtained her face and then bounced back into place as she drilled me with an expectant look from a wide-set pair of startling turquoise eyes.

When I failed to state my business, she leaned over the counter and looked around. Not seeing a four-legged creature accompanying me, she waved to a sign pointing directions to the examination rooms: "*Creatures this way—humans take a seat.*" The woman twisted her thin lips into an impish grin opening her face to life's possibilities. "You *do know* this is a *veterinary* clinic, don't you, ma'am?"

I stifled the snappy comeback on the tip of my tongue. I read the name printed on the plastic ID tag pinned to her scrubs over her left boob and beamed what I hoped was a sincere-looking hundred-thousand-watt smile. "Hello, Charlene. I'm Holly Schlivnik. My friend Ms. Lobowsky brought Sigmund, my sick standard poodle, into the clinic earlier this evening." I angled my head towards the examination room entrance. "Is the doctor available? I'd like to discuss my dog's prognosis."

Charlene nodded then made a quarter turn to reach for the phone. She took the receiver off the hook and dialed a two-digit extension. After a whispered brief conversation presumably with the vet, she motioned to a row of uncomfortable-looking plastic chairs and said, "The doctor will be right out."

Before we had a chance to sit down, the door leading to the examination rooms opened and Doogie Howser's clone stepped into the waiting room. He extended his right hand and guilelessly blinked sky-blue shiny eyes. "Doctor Jarrod Golden. I've been taking care of Sigmund. Your dog ingested quite a bit of chocolate. It's a good thing he's a standard poodle and able to tolerate such a big amount. If he was a toy poodle, he'd have likely expired. Even so, if Ms. Lobowsky didn't bring him to the clinic as quickly as she did, he might not have made it. Any idea how he got into chocolate?"

I shook my head.

He smiled reassuringly. "We've eradicated the chocolate from his system. He's understandably weak. He is stabilized, and going to be fine." Dr. Golden opened the door and waved us in. "Let's go say hello to your boy. I'm sure he'll be glad to see you. Then I'll explain his symptoms, the steps we took to eradicate the chocolate from his system, and the type of care he'll need after he is released."

Dr. Golden led us down a short hallway to the third door on the left and into a compact, well-equipped examination room. Eyes closed, Siggie lay supine—stretched out the length of the examination table. Worry lines etched octogenarian-Muriel's haggard face as she stood next to Siggie, stroking his head and speaking words of encouragement in a quiet, comforting tone. They both looked up at the sound of the door opening. My heart clenched as Siggie whimpered when he saw me and thumped his tail. I approached the table cautiously and softly scratched him in his favorite spot behind his ears. I leaned over to kiss his nose and he slurped a wet doggie kiss across my cheek.

Dr. Golden checked Siggie's vital signs and smiled at Muriel. "Would you like to take a break and join us in my office to discuss Sigmund's prognosis? If you're worried about leaving him alone, don't be. My nurse will be in his room."

Muriel shook her head. "Nah. Holly will fill me in later." Siggie licked her hand when she said, "Even if your nurse is in the room, Siggie will appreciate a familiar face hanging around."

I gave Muriel's gnarled hand an appreciative squeeze and followed Dr. Golden and Miguel out of the examination room.

****

Miguel and I sat across from Dr. Golden seated behind a scratched gunmetal gray metal desk that had seen better days.

Doctor Golden asked, "Are you familiar with the symptoms of canine chocolate poisoning?" We conveyed our ignorance with a shake of our heads and Golden continued. "Clinical signs depend on the amount and type of chocolate ingested. For many dogs, the most common clinical signs are vomiting and diarrhea, increased thirst, panting or restlessness, excessive urination, and a racing heart rate." I winced as he said, "Sigmund experienced all of these when he arrived at the clinic."

He opened Siggie's chart and referred to his notes. "Treatment of chocolate ingestions largely revolves around managing gastrointestinal signs and controlling any cardiovascular and neurologic stimulation. We administered an anti-emetic to control his excessive vomiting. A fluid diuresis allowed him to urinate frequently and helped eliminate the toxins at a faster rate. Fluids addressed dehydration and electrolyte abnormalities to avoid the secondary to vomiting or diarrhea. Sinus tachycardia is the most common arrhythmia of canine chocolate intoxication. We got lucky. Since Siggie responded well to treatment, his heart rate didn't remain high, so a beta-blocker such as propranolol wasn't needed."

I breathed a sigh of relief. "Can I bring him home?"

Golden shook his head. "His condition is stable, but I want to keep Sigmund overnight to test him for residual chocolate in his system. Call the vet on duty mid-afternoon for an update. I see no reason why you can't take Sigmund home tomorrow late afternoon. For the first two days, feed him a half-portion of his food once a day. No treats, no physical exertion, other than potty walks, keep him inside, quiet, and hydrated."

Chapter Twenty-Six

It took some doing, but Doctor Golden finally convinced Muriel Siggie was in competent hands and the best thing she could do for him was to take care of herself by going home and getting some rest.

Relieved Siggie was on the road to recovery, we three were famished. We stopped at Tiny Naylor's—a twenty-four-hour coffee shop—located at the intersection of Lincoln Blvd. and Admiralty Way. After our repast, we followed Muriel back to Porto Paloma Marina. A wave of sadness washed over me as I opened the forward door to my suddenly silent-as-a-cemetery houseboat.

Despite the stress and length of the day, Miguel and I still ran on a mixture of an adrenaline rush and nervous energy and found ourselves surprisingly wide awake. I brewed a pot of coffee and we sat across from one another in the breakfast nook of the galley rehashing the chain of events Muriel detailed leading to Siggie's getting sick.

I scrunched my eyes in concentration, trying to make some sense of it. "Muriel fed Siggie his fancy meal at the same time she fixed herself dinner around five-thirty. She didn't have enough of his regular dog food for his breakfast, so she and Siggie went back to the houseboat at six to refurbish her supply. Siggie stayed out on the forward deck while Muriel packed dog food, extra treats, and a couple of his favorite toys. She said she was inside the houseboat for ten minutes and then they went directly back to her boat. And a half-hour later, Siggie became violently ill."

Miguel stroked his chin. "So, someplace between Muriel's boat and yours is where Siggie found the chocolate. For all we know, one of your neighbors dropped a few pieces of candy by accident out of a grocery bag onto the dock."

I shook my head. "Muriel didn't say Siggie stopped between my boat and hers. She'd have taken the chocolate away from him."

"Okay, but Muriel can't account for Siggie's activity during the ten minutes she was inside the houseboat. She said Siggie wasn't on a leash. Maybe he got bored waiting for her and wandered around the dock exploring. The chocolate could have been found anyplace from the top of the gangplank all the way down the walkway back to Muriel's boat."

Fingers of dread tied my heartstrings into sailor's knots as the terrifying memory of Michael Chennault's implied threat reverberated inside my head. As a boater renting a slip in our marina, he has a key that like all tenants, *including mine*, opens *every* security gate. Saturday there wasn't a cloud in the sky, and still enough wind to make any boater happy. I bet most of my dock neighbors took advantage of the gorgeous day. Michael could plant the chocolate on my boat and none of my neighbors would be around to question him. Michael must be responsible for Siggie getting sick. I flexed my fingers, imagining how wonderful it would feel to strangle the life out of the bastard for hurting my dog.

I didn't relish telling Miguel about Michael's threat, but I had no choice. I took a fortifying glug of coffee and said, "This was no accident."

Miguel's lips were drawn into a thin line and his arms stretched tightly akimbo across his broad chest as I recounted the tale—all of it. Dawn broke as I finished. Fury blazed in Miguel's obsidian eyes as his words dripped sarcastically. "And it never *once ever* occurred to you to tell *me any* of this?"

It took every ounce of control I had not to laugh in his face. "Tell you *what?* The new owner of a company I worked at got pissed I left? Or a competitor was furious his company got kicked out of the biggest, most powerful store in LA and he went postal when I received the lion's share of his lost business? And then he made a veiled threat to hurt my dog?" I defiantly jutted my chin. "And if I did tell you? So, freaking what? Your response? *Nothing could be done until he made good on the threat and it could be proven he was responsible for the deed.*"

Miguel's shoulders slumped and the anger leeched out of his eyes. He had the grace to blush. He stood up and looked around the galley. "Do you have any plastic sandwich bags?"

"Planning a picnic?"

He clucked his tongue and flicked a wrist toward the forward door. "Maybe later. Right now, we're gonna search this boat from stem to stern for the proof. If we find it, we put it in those sandwich bags and send it to the lab."

****

Three hours later Miguel called his counterpart at the LA County Sheriff's Department to report the crumpled four chocolate candy wrappers I'd found carelessly wedged between the forward deck lock box and the hull rim now safely ensconced inside plastic sandwich bags. Ten minutes later, three LA County Sheriff's Department patrol cars screeched to a halt in front of my basin. Two officers spoke to Miguel and me while two others searched the boat. Then two-crime lab techs confiscated the plastic lunch bags. They covered the forward deck, guardrails, furniture, and lockbox with a coating of black fingerprint dust and wrapped wide strands of yellow crime scene tape around the houseboat. Cripes, I'll never get rid of all that black, grainy, dust crap.

The deputies finished their work and admonished me not to board the boat until they officially cleared it. And that will be…who knows when? Only ten a.m. Sunday morning, and I was already homeless. Add a dog recovering from a near-fatal attack to the mix and both of us needed a place to sleep and there were the makings of a rip-snorter of a crappy day.

Staying on the houseboat wasn't an option. Neither was bunking at Muriel's on a boat cozy for one and cramped for two. Checking into the hotel Queenie Levine was the obvious solution, but I couldn't bear to relive the last two days by having to re-tell my pal the whole story in the excruciating detail she would demand.

I made arrangements for Muriel to pick up Siggie after he was discharged and followed Miguel back to his house. A hot shower and a pot of strong coffee brought us back from the nearly-dead. We spent the rest of Sunday collapsed in bed.

****

Early Monday morning I kissed Miguel goodbye and headed back to the marina. By now Queenie must be fuming—bordering on furious—I hadn't called her yet. The sun rose as I crossed the intersection of Washington Street and Lincoln Blvd. I checked the time—six a.m. on the nose. I called Queenie and prepared for the ensuing verbal assault. On a good day, this is *not* a morning person. Calling Little Miss Sunshine at the crack of dawn on a *Monday*, no less ought to be a barrel of laughs— only if passing a kidney stone is your idea of a party-hardy good time.

I cringed as she answered on the fourth ring. Before inquiring who was calling, she growled in a deep voice thickened by interrupted slumber. "What moron calls before *even God* is awake? Somebody *better* be dead or whoever you are, *you will* be."

"Queenie, it's me, Holly. Sorry to call so early…"

Fully awake and firing on all pistons, the divine Ms. Levine snapped like a cranky turtle. "So, you *finally* decided to grace me by your presence. And *only two days* after the fact. Must have been one helluva a party."

If she only knew.

"Brew a pot of coffee and put the cats in the garage. I'll be at your house in fifteen minutes." I hit the off button before she could either object or lob one of her well-honed snarky replies.

After a quick pitstop for a piping-hot peace offering at Bertha's twenty-four-hour drive-through Bagel Bonanza, I turned south off Washington onto Queenie's Street. Miraculously, I snagged the only open spot not requiring a parking permit sticker a mere two blocks from Queenie's house. I grabbed the bag of bagels and my overnight bag, locked the car, and sprinted the two blocks to Queenie's front door.

Hoping for some levity to mitigate Queenie's early

morning prickliness, I rang the bell and sang in my best delivery boy falsetto. "*Bertha's Bagel Bonanza*—special delivery for Ms. Queenie Levine. Get 'em while they're still hot." The door opened and five perfectly manicured fingers reached out and snatched the bag of bagels out of my hand. I winced as I shoved my foot in the doorjamb as Miss Warm and Fuzzy tried to slam the door in my face.

I followed the scent of brewing coffee into the kitchen and found a bathrobe-clad Queenie sporting a bad case of bedhead hair waving a fat cinnamon raisin bagel under my nose. "Since you brought Bertha's Bagels, I *might* not kill you." She spotted my overnight bag and batted her eyes. "Sorry, the only roommates I accept are of the four-legged variety who meow."

I poured two cups of coffee and handed her one. "Drink up. You're gonna need it." I recounted in painstaking detail the events of the last two days. Queenie's eyes filled when I got to Siggie's chocolate poisoning fiasco. "Bastard. It takes a special kind of monster to hurt an animal. Whoever is responsible for this, should rot in Hell...if I don't get to them first...if I do, Hell is gonna look mighty inviting by comparison."

Chapter Twenty-Seven

The Yentas sat transfixed as I repeated the details of the weekend festivities. Good gravy, this sad tale of woe is already shopworn, yet the list of interested parties is as long as my arm. I might as well record the story on my smartphone and hit the start button.

Snip and AJ must be busting a gut by now wondering whether Miguel and I eloped, broke up, or killed one another after the party. And Goddess forbids if my extraordinarily overprotective parents somehow get a sniff of this debacle? Oy vey. Just shoot me.

Joan quipped, "So, Mrs. Lincoln, other than that, did you enjoy the play?"

Hope's eyes filled. "How does *anyone*, even a lowlife like Michael Chennault, *purposely* hurt an animal?"

Gimme-the-facts-ma'am Sonia stroked her chin. "What happens next?"

I fanned my fingers. "We wait for the test lab results." The peanut gallery emitted an annoying collective groan as I surveyed the table and grinned. "Of course, we all know patience has *never* been one of my strong suits…"

Joan pursed her lips. "Okay, Nancy Drew, what bonehead scheme is percolating in your meddlesome mind now?"

I sniffed with righteous indignation. "I resemble your tacky remark."

Queenie tapped her index finger on the tip of her nose and spoke as though I wasn't sitting at the same table. "She's currently a guest at the Hotel Levine. For everyone's mental health, maybe I should lock her in the guestroom until all this craziness passes."

Still currently homeless, I bit back the nasty retort on the tip of my tongue. "Even if I possessed the patience of Job, the test results might still come back a big goose egg." I looked over at Hope as she nodded her confirmation. "Michael Chennault has never been arrested. So, unless he was in the military, his fingerprints would not be in the law enforcement database. Since no physical evidence tied him to the crime scene, the cops had no probable cause. If he doesn't volunteer to, the police can't compel him to give his fingerprints. Refusal to comply makes him look guilty as hell, but I doubt he gives a rat's ass."

Sonia nodded in agreement. "She's right. The police couldn't place me at the scene of the crime when I was accused of murdering Bunny Frank because my fingerprints didn't match."

I used a teaspoon to tap a rat-a-tat-tat beat on my coffee cup. "Since fingerprints from the crime scene won't identify the perp, I've been thinking…"

Queenie closed her eyes and shivered. "Dear Goddess above please help us. Those are the three most dangerous words in the English language."

I gave her the middle finger salute and soldiered on. "I did some research on the candy company. *Le Ultra Chocolate* is an exclusive, expensive Swiss chocolate."

Hope asked, "And the cost of the candy helps

identify the perp?"

I nodded. "Yes. It narrows down the number of people who buy it."

Hope wrinkled her brow. "So?"

I held out my hands. "So, it also narrows the number of retailers who sell it. According to the company website, only a dozen candy retailers in LA sell that brand of chocolate. One of them is Bainbridge Department Stores."

Joan pursed her lips. "And?"

"And the husband of the Bainbridge *candy department buyer* and I go to the same stamp dealer." I glanced around the table. Nothing but blank stares. I swallowed my annoyance with a glug of coffee. "Don't you remember? *I told you guys about this.* The wife's got a major burr up her butt over Sue Ellen for allegedly stealing the swimwear job from her. Lois Flynn certainly has access to the chocolate. Maybe she and the killer are in cahoots. She provides the candy and the killer takes out my dog in the hopes of scaring me off my investigation. Or, even if Lois isn't involved, she still runs the department. Maybe some uber-rich person orders the chocolate through her regularly? Or a chocoholic employee who has a yen for the good stuff buys it using the company discount? If Lois can't or won't give me the information, Ms. Markowitz might be able to find out."

Joan raised her eyebrows. "Going to Cleveland by way of Cairo on this one, aren't you?

I grinned. "My dad's from Cleveland. I hear it's nice this time of year."

****

I dropped off samples at the In Style buying office

after lunch. Since I walked past Bainbridge to get back to the mart, I called Lois Flynn on the way.

"Hello, Ms. Flynn? We don't know each other. Your husband and I buy stamps from the same dealer. Darren and I met at Mr. Albin's store not long ago. I am…"

She interrupted my introduction saying she knew who I was. Hmm. I asked to meet with her in a few minutes and she readily agreed. Oddly, she didn't ask why.

Fifteen minutes later I rapped on the half-open door to Lois Flynn's cramped office. A stick-thin blonde about Sue Ellen's age batting luminous emerald eyes looked up from a computer report and waved me in. The heady scent of chocolate filled my nose and made my mouth water as I entered the wet dream of every sweet-toothed fiend on the planet.

All business now, Lois looked up at the wall clock to her left. "I've got a meeting with my boss in fifteen minutes. I'll give you five." She folded her hands in front of her and gave me an expectant look. "So, what can I do for you, Ms. Schlivnik?"

"I'm curious…given the high price, do you sell a lot of Le Ultra Chocolate?"

Lois slit her eyes. "Lemme get this straight. Le Ultra Chocolate sales… *This is* why you asked to see me?"

I put my hands out in supplication. "Not exactly."

Lois tapped the face of her wristwatch. "The clock's ticking. You've got four minutes to spit it out."

"Somebody tried to kill my dog by leaving chocolate around for him to eat. The wrappers the police found on my houseboat were Le Ultra Chocolate."

She guilelessly batted her eyes. "Dreadful to say the least. What's it got to do with me?"

"I did some research about the company and found out only a dozen stores in LA sell the brand, including Bainbridge."

Lois pursed her lips. "And?"

"And since the distribution is so narrow, it should help identify the perp."

Lois widened her eyes. "You planning on hunting down *every person in LA* who eats Le Ultra Chocolate?" She snorted her derision. "Good luck." Lois waggled her digits in the air. "Unless the person wore gloves, fingerprints will be on the wrapper."

Appreciate the heads up, Dick Tracy.

"That's true, but it's only helpful if the fingerprints on the wrappers belong to someone who has a police record. If not, then the police can't match them to a suspect." I pointed to the fancy Le Ultra Chocolate display. "So, humor me...do you have any customers who buy that specific chocolate candy regularly? Maybe some rich person who can afford to indulge themselves? Or a corporate account—a company that gives extravagant gifts to major customers. The store gives employee discounts, right? So, maybe an employee loves the brand—and if they take advantage of the company discount, they can afford to splurge." I pointed to the open computer report on her desk. "Any high unit sales spikes in that chocolate the last say, sixty days?"

Lois held out her hands. "Even if I wanted to, privacy laws prohibit me from giving you the information."

I pursed my lips. "Or maybe the reason you won't reveal the information hits a lot closer to home. Darren shared your history with Sue Ellen Magee. If she's behind bars, maybe Sue Ellen got her just desserts, and at last, you'd get the job always rightfully yours." Lois paled. "Sue Ellen is a major pain in the patootie, but she's no more a killer than me. Maybe you heard through the grapevine I'm working hard to find the real killer. Say the killer knows your history with Sue Ellen and approaches you to consider a win-win proposition to keep the Queen of Mean in jail: You do your part by providing the chocolate to the killer who scares me off my investigation by poisoning my dog."

Lois smiled sardonically. "Such a lovely little fairytale. Thanks for stopping by to share it. An entertaining yarn is always a great way to break up a boring day." Lois gathered a stack of computer reports and stood. She pointed a stubby finger at the open door. "Now if you'll excuse me, I have a meeting to attend."

I've gotta hand it to her. I threw one heck of a serious accusation out and hit her right between the eyes with it. Lois might be wetting her panties, but she put her game face on and kept her cool. Either ice water flows through her veins or she's innocent. Toss a coin. And if Sue Ellen is gonna get sprung from the hoosegow sometime before the end of this decade, I better find out which way the coin was tossed and fast. Another *"Schlivnik adventure"* is definitely in the future. I can hardly wait to tell Queenie. Won't she be tickled pink?

Chapter Twenty-Eight

Along with our partner and head designer, Gary
Burkett, and Mira Kumar, our cover-up designer,
Queenie and I spent the next morning in the showroom
working with Queenie's friend and the Bainbridge
Fashion and Trends Director, Dixie Chandler, and her
assistant Kate. Dixie and Kate were shopping the
Bainbridge major swimwear suppliers for a preview of
the silhouettes, fabrications, colors, and trends forecast
for the summer season.

Queenie, Dixie, Kate, and I sat together at the larger
of the workstations facing Gary and Mira, standing in
front of a grid adjacent to a rack packed with samples.

Gary merchandised the four major missy fashion
trends on the grid back to a sample of every pattern and
colorway, as well as solid colors going back to the prints.
Once Gary finished, Mira fit in matching printed as well
as solid cover-up styles to complete the presentation.

Gary stood to the side so Dixie and Kate had a full
view of the way the prints, solids, and bodies all worked
together. "When we were putting the line together, our
game plan was to take the four key fashion trends—
animal prints, ethnics, florals, and geometrics—and
present the styles in two groups merchandised together
with the solid color stories as the common thread binding
the trends together." He pointed to the styles on the grid.

"So, in this collection animal prints and ethnics are merchandised together and florals and geometrics in a common color story. Depending on floor space limitations, retailers can either display the trends merchandised this way or separately."

Gary waved a take-it-away gesture and Kumar fingered a solid gauze big shirt and capri pants merchandised back to the animal and ethnic trend groups. "We created a collection of bodies in solid fabrics to work in all the swimwear groups. We also used both woven and knit fabrics traditionally in the sportswear market. We designed silhouettes that can be worn right from the swimming pool to the carpool."

Queenie held up her left hand and pointed to her watch. "Since you guys have dedicated the entire day to our lines, why don't you join us for lunch? Then we come back to the mart and do juniors this afternoon."

Gary, Kumar, and Kate begged off lunch and promised to be back for the junior presentation.

****

The Blue China Moon Café across the street from the mart was mobbed as usual. Thank the Goddess, the hostess recognized Queenie and me as "frequent flyers." She pulled three menus from a plastic container adjacent to the cash register and seated us at a table in a cozy alcove in the back, far from the noisy din in the main dining room.

Dixie grabbed a handful of fried won-ton straws. "These things are addictive and not exactly low fat. Good thing I'm playing pickleball tonight and will work off this big meal." She swatted the air with an imaginary paddle. "Do you guys play?"

I shook my head. "Nope. I'm a walker. I live on a

houseboat. My dog and I do a loop around our marina and then walk to the Washington Street pier and back every morning."

Dixie tapped a chopstick in front of Queenie. "And you? As I recall, you're quite an athlete—tennis, golf, and yoga—right?"

Queenie formed her arms like an imaginary golf club and took an air swing. "I play in a golf foursome on Sunday mornings and do pilates two nights a week."

Dixie said, "The Bainbridge Employees Association formed a pickleball league a few months ago. We play on Wednesday evenings and Saturday mornings at Echo Park. I'm paired with Lois Flynn. She's not in the apparel division, but she's been with the store forever, so maybe you've met?"

Queenie and I locked eyes.

I said, "It's a small world. I am a stamp collector and Lois' husband is too. We both buy from the same dealer in the valley. Darren and I met the last time I was in the store. I told him I was an apparel sales exec and he mentioned his wife was the Bainbridge candy department buyer. I recently met Lois."

Dixie poked an index finger into her cleavage and joked. "Are you another chocoholic?"

"No. Regrettably, someone tried to poison my dog with chocolate and accidentally dropped the wrappers on my houseboat. I contacted Lois to ask her some questions about the brand, but she couldn't or wouldn't help me out."

Dixie shivered. "Why would anyone do such an awful thing? Is your dog okay?"

"He's recovering. Thank you for asking. I've been conducting my own investigation to find the Easter

Bunny's real killer and received some threats. Hurting my dog to make me quit investigating is one of them."

Dixie arched a brow. "Maybe you ought to pay more attention to those threats."

Holy guacamole. Did this woman just threaten me in front of Queenie?

I turned to drill my partner with a *"see, I told you so"* glare, but Queenie had found something fascinating to examine on the floor.

The conversation ended when the server arrived carrying a tray loaded with heaping plates full of steaming-hot food. While we tucked into our meals in companionable quiet, disturbing thoughts I dreaded sharing with Queenie ping-ponged around in my head.

On the way back to the mart, I asked Dixie, "Are there many more vendors left for you to work with?"

She shook her head. "Nope. Now that I've seen your line, all the missy vendors are done." I barely avoided being struck by a bus mid-way across the intersection when she added, "After I see Itsy Bitsy in the morning and Ditzy in the afternoon, I'll be finished with all the junior vendors as well."

****

Sonia Wilson, our junior division president, and Gary made the junior presentation. It went quite well, but since Dixie asked to see almost all the styles on the model, the meeting took up the balance of the afternoon. Queenie and I had no opportunity to do a postmortem on our lunchtime conversation with Dixie. The day had been long and action-packed, and we were both exhausted. A Coast Pizza takeaway pie and a bottle of wine on Queenie's deck overlooking the mighty Pacific was the perfect segway to a difficult conversation.

I glugged a gulp of liquid courage and faced my friend. Hopefully, by the time this little chitty-chat is concluded, I won't find myself homeless for the second time in one week.

Industrial-sized cluck-cluck de grande me threw my pal a softball to ease her into the thorny subject. "Queenie, what are the odds of two Sue Ellen haters who work for the same company, and don't know one another, becoming pickleball partners in a league?"

Queenie Levine may be a lot of things, but asleep at the wheel isn't one of them. She narrowed her eyes to slits. "I'm not gonna like the direction you're goin' on this, am I, Hol?"

No shit, Sherlock.

I sighed. "Probably not. Come on, don't tell me the same thought didn't cross your mind."

She shook her head. "If you're suggesting Dixie Chandler and Lois Flynn conspired to destroy Sue Ellen by killing the Easter Bunny and framing the Queen of Mean for the murder, you've lost your marbles."

I clucked my tongue. "These two are so obvious, they blink like a klieg light." I counted the points on my fingers. "Motive—I can't think of two people who have stronger motives. Opportunity—They both work at Bainbridge, know Sue Ellen's schedule, and the best way to get around the security cameras. And let's face it, *no one* has better access to jelly beans than Lois Flynn."

Queenie rolled her eyes. "You left out a pretty important component. Getting their mitts on *Botox*?"

I waved her off with a flick of a wrist. "They buy it online. Then Google the lethal dosage for a human male and they're off to the races."

Queenie pursed her lips like a funnel. "And I

suppose *those two* are also responsible for poisoning Siggie? And their motive? Before today, Dixie met you once for five minutes and Lois met you *after* Siggie ate the poisoned chocolate."

"I'm pretty sure Darren ran straight home after he and I met at Mr. Albin's and filled his wife in on *everything*. He knows where I live and work, the buyer I deal with at Bainbridge, and most of all, that I believe Sue Ellen is innocent and will do my best to prove it." I raised my wineglass in a mock toast. "Enough motive for you?"

Queenie raked her fingers through her hair. "So, now Dixie and Lois are at the top of your suspect list and all of a sudden, Michael Chennault is a choirboy?"

I scratched the crown of my head. "Yes and no. Dixie and Lois look awful good for doing the deed, yet Michael would do *anything* to get Ditzy back into Bainbridge. If Dixie has an appointment to review the new Ditzy line—then apparently, Michael succeeded. I'm meeting Abby tomorrow morning to go over the first three summer deliveries. Everything in life has a price. If Ditzy is reinstated into the Bainbridge vendor matrix, I'll do my best to find out the price Michael paid and to whom."

Chapter Twenty-Nine

The next morning, I entered the Bainbridge swimwear buying office and found Abby ensconced behind Sue Ellen's desk and not at her own.

An unsettling thought invaded my addled brain. Maybe Bainbridge management didn't announce it yet, but decided to cut its losses, fire Sue Ellen, and substitute Abby Blane in her place? Then Lois Flynn will be awfully pissed that she'd been screwed a second time and still didn't get kissed.

Never one to skirt an issue, I squared my shoulders and faced Abby Blane head-on. I bit back the word *presumptuous* and settled for a slightly less combative phrasing—for me, at least. I smiled sardonically and pinwheeled my hands around the room. "A bit premature, don't you think?"

Abby had the grace to blush. "Sue Ellen is no murderer, and sooner or later the cops are gonna nail the real killer, but who knows how long it will take? Our business goes on either way." She waved a pen to the outer office. "It's too difficult to do the work from my dinky desk. The minute Sue Ellen is back, I'll gladly move back to my desk." Abby pointed to the sample crate. "Let's get to work on the first three deliveries, shall we?"

****

Two hours later, I repacked the samples into the crate and waited for Abby to give me the bulk orders I needed to put her goods onto the early delivery production schedule.

Midway through her writing, Abby raised her arms and stretched. "I dunno about you, but I need a pick-me-up." She leaned behind Sue Ellen's desk and opened a bar-sized refrigerator. She produced two frosty-cold bottles of fancy fruit-flavored carbonated water and handed me one.

I nearly spat out the first sip when Abby pulled a sample-sized box of Le Ultra Chocolates out of a desk drawer and set it between us. Abby smiled as she opened the box. "You ever eaten one of these? They're out of this world. One bite and you're spoiled. Nothing else will do." She selected one of the chocolates, unwrapped it, and popped it into her mouth. She moaned with pleasure and giggled like a naughty schoolgirl. "If not for my employee discount, these chocolates are so expensive I'd have to sell a kidney to afford them. Even with it, this dinky sampler box is all I can afford to ward off those once-a-month chocolate cravings all women get." She pushed the box toward me and laughed good-naturedly. "Go ahead. Take one. I promise I won't charge you."

I made no move to take a piece of the chocolate and Abby widened her eyes. "Don't tell me you don't like *chocolate*! My mother says it's *abnormal* for a woman not to like chocolate."

I shook my head. "No, it's not that."

She narrowed her eyes. "Then what *is* it?"

"The particular brand."

She squawked like a parrot. "The brand? What could you possibly have against *this particular* company?"

I sighed and proceeded to detail my sad story.

I finished and she curled her upper lip and spat. "Better be a special place in Hell for anyone who hurts an animal." She tapped her pinky on the candy wrapper. "I hope they catch the SOB responsible for this and throw the book at them."

I lifted a shoulder. "The crime lab is running all sorts of tests and putting the results through the system. The police are not too optimistic. If the perp has no criminal record, then nothing from the crime scene will match anything in the system. I'll let you know if anyone does." I pointed to the paperwork. "In the meantime, let's finish this up. The sooner I get these orders into the system and onto the production schedule, the faster I'll be able to confirm your delivery dates."

Since my normally stellar ability to pry information out of unwitting foils let me down, I failed to come up with a plausible way to couch the issue of Ditzy Swimwear regaining its place on the Bainbridge vendor matrix. Patience has never been one of my strong suits, yet like so many other unanswered questions in this crazy caper, I had no choice but to leave fleshing this one out for another day.

Chapter Thirty

The sheriff's detective called on my way back to the mart and said my houseboat had been released by the crime lab team. No one would be happier than Queenie's two cats to see me check out of the Hotel Levine. Despite being warned to expect it, my shoulders still slumped with disappointment when the detective reported none of the evidence or fingerprints from my houseboat matched anyone in the LA County criminal database. In case the culprit wasn't local, the crime lab also ran the test results through a statewide database. Unfortunately, the search only resulted in another goose egg.

I strode into the mart ten minutes later intending to go up to the showroom. Instead, I had a mental itch needing a scratch and made a detour. An hour later I left the Rampart Police Station mad enough to spit nails. Why did I even bother? As though doing me a gigantic favor, Gator Goodwin barely glanced up from a computer report to hear what I had to say.

"Detective, *Michael Chennault* threatened my dog, *not Sue Ellen Magee*. It makes no sense to accuse *her* since the purpose of my investigation was to *help her*, *not help you* convict her. Besides, Sue Ellen was a guest at the Graybar Hotel when Siggie ingested the poisoned chocolate. You a betting man, Detective?" I didn't give him a chance to reply. "Because if you are, the one thing you can bet the farm on is whoever poisoned my dog and knocked off the Easter Bunny is the same dirty rat, and it sure as hell *wasn't* the Queen of Mean."

I asked when he'd be releasing Sue Ellen and the detective drew his lips into a thin line of disdain. "Get real, Ms. Schlivnik. She'll be released the second Tuesday of next week."

His cavalier attitude so disgusted me, that I left without the courtesy of saying goodbye. I stomped down the hall and barged into Miguel's office. Hey, what's the point of having a police captain for a boyfriend if you can't take advantage and pull rank once in a while? Wait. Who said, *boyfriend*? A few Chinese dinners, a couple of movies, a jazz concert, some laughs watching the weirdos on the Venice boardwalk and attending a birthday party for a niece made him my boyfriend. Is he? Do I want him to be? And if the answer is yes, where does it leave me and Buddy? Overnight, I went from no man in my life to too many men in my life. Maybe Sigmund Freud Schlivnik is the only man for me.

Miguel turned a double-take when I stormed into his office. He came around his desk to hug me but I pulled out of his embrace and snapped like a cranky croc. "Despite my blowing up your crackerjack detective's timeline, he's incapable of arresting the right person." I jabbed my index finger into Miguel's chest. "Someone tried to poison my dog to scare me into giving up my investigation. Who's responsible?" My voice dripped with sarcasm. "It must be that menace to society, Sue Ellen Magee." I wagged my index finger in the air and sneered. "Oh, wait, it can't be her. Barney Fife down the hall arrested her and then threw Sue Ellen in jail. Don't you find it rather suspicious the attempt on my dog's life occurred *after* Sue Ellen Magee's arrest? *Michael Chennault, not Sue Ellen Magee*, threatened to harm Siggie to scare me off and then he followed through on it. I'm close to solving this one and the Easter Bunny's murderer is doing everything possible to stop me." I was itching for a fight and baited him. "Too bad you and your *expert* team of detectives won't pull your heads out of your asses long enough to see the *wrong person* is rotting away in jail."

To his credit and my frustration, the consummate professional Miguel Martinez kept his cool and refused to take the bait. "The police work based on facts, not emotion. And the *fact is*, absolutely *no* physical evidence ties Mr. Chennault to Siggie's poisoning or Mr. Conejo's murder. The *fact is*, *no suspect* is tied to Siggie's poisoning. *The fact is*, all the physical evidence of Mr. Conejo's murder is tied to one suspect, and the suspect is the one Detective Goodwin arrested. Sue Ellen Magee." Miguel's dark eyes turned hard as diamonds. "I'm warning you. Don't interfere in our case again."

No point in wasting any more time trying to convince him. My words fell on deaf ears. The only way this case gets solved is on my own. I squared my shoulders and turned on my heel. I stood in the doorjamb and defiantly jutted my jaw. "Since you're not gonna help me, stay out of my way. Arrest Michael Chennault when I get you the evidence. If I'm wrong, arrest me."

****

Buddy returned from the New York sportswear market week the night before and invited Siggie and me for dinner at his house the next evening. A quick change of clothes and I was ready to spend some quality time with my pup before we left for Buddy's. Seemingly fully recovered from his ordeal, Siggie did the two-legged doggie happy dance when I dangled his leash and asked if he would like to take a jaunt to the pier before we left for Buddy's house.

We crossed Palawan Way, cut diagonally through Admiralty to Washington Street, and headed west. I let Siggie off the leash midway down the pier. He scampered happily to the end and almost bowled over our fisherman friend Pop as they danced in a joyous reunion jig.

Pop scratched Siggie behind the ears and asked him, "Where in tarnation you been hiding, big fella? Mornings just aren't the same without you helpin' me fish." Pop winked at me and laughed. "And thanks to *you* disappearing, I had to fend for myself getting a cuppa Joe."

Normally, every morning at dawn Siggie and I walked around our marina twice and then made our way to the Jolt of Java coffee shop at the end of Washington Street. I bought two biggie to-go cups of coffee…one for me, and one for Pop.

A purplish vein in the center of Pop's forehead pulsed in unbridled fury by the time I finished the tale. He growled incredulously from deep in his throat. "And the *cops can't* identify the bastard?"

I shook my head.

Pop removed his faded ball cap missing a letter so it read *LA Odgers* and razed his fingernails back and forth across the silvery corkscrew knot of hair on the crown of his head. "In that case, you gotta bait the hook to catch the fish."

Huh?

"The guy you think is responsible for doin' the

deed—he don't know if he succeeded or not, right?"

I shrugged. "Dunno. A colleague of mine works for him. I never told her to keep it a secret. So?"

"You said he has a boat in Porto Paloma on the other side of the marina from your basin. Why don't you and Siggie take a walk and let him see Siggie is still alive?"

Huh? He seemed normal, but Pop spent an awful lot of time outside. Had he been out in the sun too long and it fried the old timer's brain? "And give him the chance to finish the job? No way."

Pop clucked his tongue. "Knowledge is power. You know his MO. You're on high alert now. Between you and your neighbor, mebbe you catch him in the act."

Holy guacamole.

I checked my watch and got nervous. We spent more time with Pop than we should have. Now we had to hustle our bustles to stop for a couple of bottles of wine and still get to Buddy's on time. I told Pop I'd give his idea serious consideration. Then we said our goodbyes and headed back to the marina.

As we crossed Admiralty onto Palawan Way, I consulted my hound. "Siggie, I've been thinking over Pop's suggestion." Siggie turned his big head to the side to let me know he was paying attention. "Pop is one of the smartest men we know, so I always take his ideas to heart. No question he loves you and would never suggest anything to *intentionally* put you in harm's way. Yet this one has the potential to be dangerous to your health, so we have to think this out carefully." I pointed to the apartment buildings bisecting our marina. "We either go right and walk past Michael's boat and see if he's on board, or left to our side of the marina and go straight to Buddy's. Since you're the one who would be the most at risk, you should be part of the decision. What do you think we should do?"

Siggie stopped walking and looked both ways to consider his options. He tilted his head to the right and said, "*Woof*!" He used his powerful shoulders to yank on the leash and pulled me along to the south side of the marina.

I giggled nervously as we walked closer to our destination. Good gravy…if Miguel knew what we were doing, he would blow a gasket.

Ten minutes later we arrived at Michael's basin. We stood in front of the security gate and peered in. Michael was hosing down the foredeck. He caught sight of us in his peripheral vision, and his eyes widened when he saw Siggie. Michael recovered quickly and flashed an evil grin. He gave a two-fingered salute and yelled, "Ahoy, matey. Nice to see you *both* out and about on such a beautiful day."

Yeah right. And I just signed a contract to play center on a professional basketball team.

I returned the two-fingered salute and chose not to reply to his nautical salutation. I guess Pop was right. Should I be gratified or terrified? From the weakness in my knees, maybe a little of both. For better or worse, I'd baited the hook. Gulp. As we headed to the parking structure, I made a mental note to bring Muriel up to speed.

****

The moment Buddy opened the door, my mouth watered as my nose followed the garlicky aroma of his Mee-maw's world-famous Jambalaya wafting from the kitchen. Buddy set the bag containing two bottles of wine on the living room coffee table and folded me into his

185

embrace.

I shivered when the temperature in the room suddenly dropped fifty degrees. Two familiar apparitions appeared next to me as Buddy's lips brushed mine and he talked into my hair. "Land sakes, girl, it's only been a week, yet it seems like a month of Sundays since I held you in my arms."

Marie LaValle cackled with delight and blew an icy breath into my ear. "Say hallelujah and praise Heaven above. It's about darned time!"

Buddy held me at arm's length and searched my face with concerned eyes. "You're shivering. You coming down with something?"

Oh, yeah…or *something*, all right.

I turned away so Buddy couldn't see my eyes had filled. My heart broke for him. So close and yet so far to his precious baby girl.

Snatched from him with no warning, Buddy had no idea that by the end of that fateful day, he'd never make love to his wife or hold his daughter again. So, on the one hand, how wonderful it would be if he could see and talk to his family. On the other hand, how unimaginably painful. And selfishly, it left Buddy and me…where?

Little Justine's frosty fingers tickled my dog's nose. "Mama! Look at the big doggie! May I play with him, please?" Siggie yelped as the girl-ghost jumped on his back and tried to ride him.

"No, you most certainly may not!" Marie pulled Justine off of a relieved Siggie and swatted the little girl lightly on the behind.

Buddy, of course, misunderstood why Siggie barked. Buddy bent at the knees and scratched Sig behind his ears. "Don't you worry, big guy…I didn't forget about you. You're gonna love the delicious doggy meal I planned just for you."

I sniffed the air and swooned from the aroma. "How much longer are you gonna torture me?"

Buddy grabbed the two bottles of wine and escorted me into the kitchen with Siggie trailing close behind. I filled Siggie's travel water dish and breathed a sigh of relief as Marie and Justine disappeared into thin air.

Buddy plated the jambalaya while I poured the wine and we ate the deliciously spicy concoction in companionable silence. After dinner, we did the dishes together. Then we retired to the living room along with a carafe of strong Cajun coffee and authentic beignets Buddy discovered at a new bakery on Main Street in Venice a block from the beach. Their southern-style dessert selections reminded him of Café du Monde in New Orleans. Buddy put a selection of smooth jazz CDs into the player and we settled into the sofa with Siggie contentedly sound asleep on the floor between our feet. Lucy and Ricky enjoying one another's company after a long day.

Buddy regaled me with hilarious New York sportswear market stories. Then he made the take-it-away sign with his hands. "And your week?"

A helluva lot more exciting than yours.

I took a sip of coffee to give myself a moment to couch a response. I debated whether or not to tell Buddy everything. I should have, but Buddy and Miguel already behaved like two bull moose fighting over a cow. Relating the hot mess served no purpose other than lighting a match and tossing it into a container of gasoline.

I chose a version of the truth if you squinted, and left

out a "few" pertinent details. "The usual. Organized chaos. Cranky sales reps complaining about late deliveries. Crabby buyers yammering they can't sell empty hangers. Wah, wah. The only thing that went smoothly? The presentation of our summer collections to the fashion and trend team from Bainbridge."

Buddy smiled and squeezed my shoulder. "Sounds like it was a tough week."

You have no idea, Buddy Boy.

He snapped his fingers. "I've got just the cure. Our marketing department arranged a big trunk show at The Little Daisy in San Francisco for next Sunday afternoon. All the prep work will be taken care of by the marketing team. I just show up and be the Master of Ceremonies at the two-hour event from four to six. So, there will be plenty of free time. Why don't you come with me? I've never been to San Francisco. I can't think of anyone I'd rather explore the city by the bay with than you. We can catch a late afternoon flight on Friday and arrive in time for dinner at Fisherman's Wharf."

I drank a big sip of coffee to buy myself a few moments to figure out a plausible response. In a game of mental ping pong, I reasoned after all Siggie's been through these past few days, I wanted to keep a close watch on him. It's not that I didn't trust Muriel or AJ to take good care of my boy. The problem is with the possibility of another threat from Michael looming over our heads, I'm not comfortable leaving Siggie. Yeah, right…Even to my ears, the lame excuse sounded like enough baloney to build a double-decker sandwich. The truth? That pile of hooey was nothing more than a piss-poor pretext to justify my hesitation to take the next big step in our relationship. Nonetheless, Buddy asked a question that deserved a response. Oy vey.

I glanced surreptitiously around the room for Marie and Justine to reappear as Buddy gathered me snugly into his arms. Mercifully, we appeared alone. I grew heady from his citrusy cologne as a voice sounding suspiciously like mine hoarsely whispered, "I'd love to."

Chapter Thirty-One

I distributed the round of coffee to the Yentas the next morning and filled them in on the latest events…well, maybe most of them. The Yentas' reaction to a couple of ghosts popping up willy-nilly to encourage me to drop-kick Miguel to the curb and marry Buddy is not one I cared to consider.

Joan grinned evilly and then gave me a round of applause. "Congratulations. Despite your best efforts, you miraculously managed to get through a couple of days keeping all your body parts and houseboat still intact."

Queenie smacked the table with the heel of her hand. "For crying out loud, Joan! Don't give it the evil eye." She pointed a teaspoon at me. "The week is still young. Plenty of time for Nancy Drew to get herself into a world of trouble."

Hope clucked her tongue. "Your friend Pop is right about one thing. Knowledge *is* power. And that's why I purposely said *nothing* to Michael regarding Siggie. Pop did you no favor giving such dangerous advice. And then you stupidly follow it and goad Michael by prancing your dog in front of his boat." She sighed. "Good grief, Holly. For a smart woman, you sure make some bonehead decisions—and this is one you might pay for with your life."

I bunched my shoulders. "Michael is in the marina almost every day. Sooner or later, we'd run into him someplace. This way we controlled where and when the encounter took place and had the element of surprise in our favor. I gauged his guilt or innocence by the way he reacted when he saw Siggie on the dock." I surveyed the table. "The SOB was utterly stunned. My neighbors Muriel and Mark, the ex-Navy SEAL who lives on the boat next to mine, are on watch duty. Trust me, Michael Chennault will not get past either of them."

Sonia absently twisted a wisp of her dirty blonde hair into a knot. "Do you honestly think Michael will make a second attempt?"

Hope sighed. "No question about it. Yes. This is a power-hungry man who will never give up until he gets what he wants."

I jutted my jaw. "I'm counting on it. *Nobody* tries to hurt my dog and gets away with it. I am gonna nail Michael Chennault's sorry ass to the wall." I held out my hands. "The key to nailing Michael is the candy wrappers."

Sonia wrinkled her brow. "Why? If his fingerprints are on them and don't match any in the system, why do the wrappers matter?"

"All the cops need is probable cause to compel Michael to give his fingerprints. And I've got just the person who can provide the information to the cops. I'm gonna visit her later today."

****

I checked my watch. Crap on a crumpet. It was way past late. I'd spent a lot more time than I planned to at the Acme Buying Office—the storied, stuffy, and most prestigious buying office in LA—making a presentation to the CEO of their biggest client—Jethro Barnes, the head honcho of Diamond's Department Stores. I'd planned a narrowly-focused presentation featuring only our best retailing items hoping to entice him enough to add our lines onto the store vendor matrix next season. The presentation went extremely well and fingers crossed, we had a good shot of getting all our divisions into Diamond's.

As I packed up my sample crate, Barnes asked if we had any goods for immediate delivery. He desperately needed goods to replace units another supplier failed to deliver. Even a big chain like Diamond's can't sell empty hangers.

In a seasonal business like ours, if you snooze you lose, as there is no second season to make up for any lost sales. Diamond's is a huge, powerful retailer every vendor covets selling to. For a supplier to disappoint an important account like Diamond's is a case of unforgivable industry negligence.

Never one to squander an opportunity, especially if it smacks you in the face and says pay attention, dummy, I sprang into action. Hopefully, the other supplier's mistake will be our ticket into Diamonds. I called Ike, our production guy at the factory. Four groups of fabulous styles a contractor double cut by mistake hung in our warehouse available to ship the next day.

Ike faxed me the inventory and CADS of the available styles. Barnes loved the selection. Hallelujah! He wrote the order right then and I called it into Queenie. The good news? Barnes announced if Mermaid delivered everything as promised, we would be replacing the other supplier. The bad news? It was late—way past quitting time for most buyers. Now I'm forced to sprint down

Main Street and pray Lois Flynn was working past quitting time.

****

The ancient Bainbridge elevator shuddered to a stop on the executive floor. The buying office cube configuration comprised of two wings anchored by the senior management offices in the middle. The south wing housed all the soft goods buyers—all apparel, intimate apparel, shoes, outerwear, jewelry, accessories, handbags, cosmetics, towels, linens, and the fashion and trends departments. The north wing housed all the hardline goods buyers—furniture, housewares, small appliances, fine and informal china, cutlery, silverware, luggage, cosmetics, and candy.

My heart sank as I made my way down the dark corridor of the north wing to Lois Flynn's small, cramped office—the last one on the aisle. All the outer office doors I passed on the way to Lois's office were closed. Since I was already there, just for the heck of it, I twisted the handle of Lois's outer door and remarkably, it opened. All the lights were on, and it appeared Lois had not left for the day. I stepped through the outer door and rapped a rat-a-tat-tat on the three-quarter-closed-door of Lois's office. No response. I put a lot more elbow grease into it the second time and still got the big goose egg for my trouble. For giggles and squeaks, I knocked a third time, and still nada.

The good manners my mother raised me with said you don't barge in uninvited. Patience has never been one of my strong suits and hanging around forever wasn't an option. After three minutes of waiting for an epiphany and my thumb up my ass while contemplating my choices, I said screw the good manners and opened the door.

Lois Flynn's stiff-as-a-board body lay bent in half over her desk. Her chin rested on the edge of her blotter. I passed a hand in front of her mouth. She wasn't breathing.

Her rigid arms stretched out on the desk in front of her, fists tightly clenched. She appeared to be holding something. I leaned in for a closer look. She clutched a piece of wrapped *Le Ultra Chocolate* between the index finger and thumb of her right hand. I turned a visual tour around the room. My heart banged against my ribcage when I spied a couple of crumpled candy wrappers on the floor next to Lois's desk. Were the candy wrappers carelessly strewn by a killer in a hurry or did Lois have a sudden chocolate craving? Only an autopsy will tell.

Her sightless eyes stared wide open from either fright or surprise at her situation. No kidding. That made two of us. Either way, there was no need for an MD to be written after my name to make this diagnosis. Dead-as-a-doornail Lois Flynn had placed her last purchase order. I swallowed my usual nervous reaction of laughing whenever I encountered a corpse and instead, whispered a little prayer.

I went back into the outer office and plopped my weary bones into the only guest chair. I pulled Glory Washington's business card out of my messenger bag and punched her numbers into my cell phone. I checked my watch. By the time I gave the cops my statement, this was gonna be a super late night. I called Muriel and asked her to take care of Siggie overnight.

Twenty minutes later Glory, Gator, and a flotilla of LAPD uniforms crammed themselves into Lois's tiny office. Ten minutes after the cops arrived, Los Angeles

County Assistant Coroner Sophie Cutler and her crew came in, carrying a gurney and a large assortment of crime scene paraphernalia. The motley group danced their way into the festivities in the corpse-cutter conga line that had become all too familiar.

Since I came in as they say, at the end of the movie, I had nothing particularly helpful to offer. I promised to go to the Rampart Police Station the next day to sign my formal statement, and they let me leave.

Chapter Thirty-Two

The Bainbridge security guard ushered me out of the employee entrance at the back of the store. I'd come and gone into the store via the employee entrance countless times, but never in the dark. The bank of timed security lights over the store entrance did little to calm my nerves. After the guard locked the door behind me, the outside lights automatically turned off. I stood in the dark rooted to the spot—too scared to leave and more frightened not to go.

I put my virtual big girl panties on, tightened my grip on the messenger bag strap, and kept my eyes focused downward to ignore the shadows of the huge trash disposal units lining the alley. During the day they stood tall as sentries. Shrouded by darkness, they appeared like monsters under the bed when a child had a bad dream. I took a calming breath and high-stepped it down the alley triple-time. I glanced over my shoulder every thirty seconds expecting to encounter—who knows?

Miraculously, I made it to the end of the alley intact and turned onto Main Street. Other than two scruffy-looking guys too busy sharing a joint to notice me, I was the only one on the street. No one to help me if I got into trouble, but at least the street was well-lit. I made all the green lights and arrived unscathed at the California

Apparel Mart in record time.

I entered the building and took the elevator down to the second floor of the parking structure. The convertible was the only car on the floor. I eyeballed the garage for anyone lurking behind the elevator bank. No one jumped out, so I raced to my car.

I no sooner planted my derrière into the well-worn leather driver's seat and locked the doors and my cell phone rang. The caller ID said Captain Miguel Martinez. Good gravy, that didn't take long. Apparently, Glory Washington couldn't wait for me to get as far as the elevator before she called her boss to fink on me.

Crap on a crumpet. A perfect end to a perfect evening. My first reaction? Let it ring and ignore him. I needed another lecture like I needed a second tush. On second thought—a terrible decision. If Glory told Miguel what time I left the store and I wasn't answering my phone, the good Captain would think the worst and send the cavalry out to save me. Then I'd be in even hotter water than I already was.

I pressed the on button and braced myself. Good thing. My favorite cop didn't disappoint. If I left the cell phone in the car and went back up to the mart lobby, I'd still be able to hear him loud and clear. *"Are you just determined to get yourself killed or do you not understand English? Let me make this crystal clear for you. If you continue to stick your nose where it doesn't belong, I will have you arrested for interference in an official murder investigation!"*

I opened my mouth to tell him to take his old nightstick and where to shove it. Unfortunately, the buzzing of the dial tone said I'd be keeping the suggestion to myself until another time.

I put the top down and cranked the radio up to a deafening level and aimed the convertible west on I-10. Traffic was comparatively light for once on the 405 southbound and I made it to the 90 west in record time. My growling tummy sent out a loud complaint that the chef's salad lunch was now only a distant memory. Too exhausted to fix something at home and for once in my life, not in the mood for takeaway pizza, I pulled into the Tiny Naylor parking lot.

While waiting for the Denver omelet to be served, I sipped my coffee and ran the events of the last few days through my mind. Who poisoned Pedro Conejo? Who poisoned Siggie? Who murdered Lois Flynn? By me, all three deeds were done by the same person. The question is who? But until I figured out the *why*, the killer's identity would remain a mystery. What do the TV detectives always say? *Follow the money.* Queenie always asked, "Who had the most to lose?" No matter which routes I traveled down, all roads still led to Michael Chennault.

****

After ten p.m. the security guard pulls the grid down and locks the main entrance to the Porto Paloma Marina subterranean parking structure and reopens it at six am. Between those hours, tenants use the auxiliary entrance on the side of the marina opposite mine. Michael Chennault's basin is diagonally across from the secondary parking structure entrance. As I made the turn, I noted the lights blazed brightly on Michael's boat.

Thankfully, Muriel took Siggie for the night. I love my hound, but I'd simply run out of the energy needed to entertain him. All I wanted? To get horizontal and try to erase the vision of Lois Flynn's rigid corpse splayed over her desk from my memory.

I reached over the forward guard rail and dropped my messenger bag onto the deck. I planted one foot on the dock and the other one on the deck. When I grabbed the guard rail to hoist myself over, it pulled completely out of the fittings. One foot on and one foot off, my stride was too short to recover. I had nothing to hold onto and screamed loud enough to wake up the dead. I fell into the cold, murky water and slipped between the dock and my boat.

The momentum of the boat pushed me against the dock. I scraped against the barnacles and tore my blazer and new gabardine trousers to shreds. The water turned a pinkish red and I prayed sharks don't swim this far into the marina. I powered up using my knees as leverage and pushed out against the hull. Thanks to the help of low tide, I moved the boat enough to slither out and free myself.

I shivered as something slimy swam between my feet after I kicked off my shoes so as not to sink like a rock. It proved impossible to get my bearings in the dark, murky water. I felt my way around the hull like a blind guy playing hide-and-seek. I reached up to the juncture of the hull and the forward deck and found the bow line tethering my boat to the cleat horn. A half-dozen attempts to hoist myself out of the water proved futile because the oily sludge from the channel water coating my hands made it impossible to get a grip on the line.

Exhaustion leeched the last reserves of my energy. As I started to fade, a blinding light blurred my vision and a familiar voice commanded, "I see her, Mark! She's on the port side of the forward deck maybe five feet from the cleat horn. You can reach her if you lay down on the dock and stretch as far as you can."

Just as I started to sink, two strong arms reached under my armpits and pulled me onto the dock.

Siggie never left my side as Muriel swathed me like a newborn with thermal blankets and pushed a seat cushion under my head. Twenty minutes later I stopped shivering and sat up so Muriel could examine my wounds. My shredded clothes took the brunt of my brush with the barnacles. Muriel cleaned my superficial scrapes, applied an antiseptic, bandaged the wounds, and insisted I get them checked out by a doctor in the morning.

Mark handed me a steaming cup of hot coffee. I took a restorative gulp and pointed to the collapsed rail guard. "I climb over the same rail guard daily, sometimes several times a day, and never so much as a slight loosening. And now, out of the clear blue, it comes completely out of the fittings."

Mark and Muriel shared a look.

Mark said, "It didn't."

I snapped to attention. "Whaaat?"

Mark took a grappling hook out of his dock box then attached the claw to the aft port side guard rail of my boat and gave it a gentle tug. To my horror, the guard rail came out of the fittings the same way as the forward one.

"This is nuts. I pay a bucket of bucks every month to fastidiously maintain her. She underwent a complete inspection not three weeks ago and passed with flying colors."

Mark shook his head. "This isn't a result of neglect or wear and tear. Screw marks are on all the fittings. This is no accident. Your boat has been tampered with. Someone with boating knowledge loosened all the fittings."

****

The psychedelic light shows the emergency vehicles flashing strobe bubbles created an eerie specter as they bounced off the walls of the apartment buildings across from my basin. Two LA County Sheriff's officers kept my dock neighbors at a distance from my houseboat now swathed by yellow crime scene tape.

Fanfreakingtastic. Must be some kind of record—even for me. Homeless for the second time in a week.

After the cops arrived, Antonio, the security guard, called the dockmaster to bring her up to speed. Twenty minutes later, Dock Mistress Audrey Camarillo arrived at my boat slip.

The Los Angeles Sheriff's Department detective asked, "Any idea who is responsible?"

I motioned to the gate above the gangplank. "You need a key to get into the basins. Every tenant has a key to the gate and their key works on all the gates in the marina. I'm not saying boaters don't let outsiders in, because we all do. But this time of night? I doubt if a boater is still out, and if someone is, they certainly wouldn't let a stranger in."

Audrey shrank back in horror. "You're saying one of *our tenants* is responsible?"

I nodded. "Yeah, and I have a pretty good idea which one. He was aboard his boat tonight."

I did a double-take as Miguel purposely strode down the gangplank and stopped at my slip. He put his arm protectively around my shoulders, but I wriggled out of his grasp.

"How did you find out something bad was going on here?"

He grinned. "That's why they call me a detective." His lame attempt at levity fell flat, so he went with the truth. "My friend at the sheriff's department saw the call come in with your name on it and texted me."

I was in no mood for his ill-timed humor and I needed another lecture like I needed a migraine. "Why are you here? Did you forget a few jabs from your earlier diatribe and wanted to get the rest of them in?"

He flinched as though he'd been struck. "N-no, of course not. I was worried sick over you." He pointed to my houseboat swathed by crime scene tape. "You can't stay on the boat. I'll talk to the detective and ask if he'll allow you to pack a few things. You and Siggie can stay at my place until the boat is released."

When pigs fly, Mickey.

"No thanks. Siggie will be happier staying at Muriel's and I'll be more comfortable at a hotel."

****

By the time I finished getting Siggie settled in at Muriel's and giving the detective my statement, my wristwatch read way past Why bother going to sleep O'clock? The deputy sheriff generously gave me a whole five minutes to board the boat and pack an overnight bag. The right thing to do was to check into a hotel, but after the events of the last few days, I didn't relish the idea of being alone. Far from being an early riser, I'd scare the pants off Queenie if I called her in the middle of the night. However, Snip is another story. My favorite coroner rose daily at four-thirty a.m. for a 5-mile run she swore mitigated her atrocious eating habits.

****

The delicious scent of coffee brewing wafted through the kitchen to the hallway when I knuckle-rapped once and opened Snip's front door. I entered her cozy kitchen and slid into a 50s-style vinyl chair in front of a round Formica table made shiny with age. Already dressed in her running clothes, long and lean Snip bent in half to deliver a hug. She pivoted to the counter and handed me a ceramic coffee mug. The face of the mug featured a cartoon of a covered corpse lying on a gurney and a toe tag sticking out. The caption read: *Coroners do it lying down.*

Snip sat across the table and observed me over the rim of her coffee mug. "No offense pal—my patients look livelier than you."

Who says medical examiners lack a sense of humor?

I smiled sardonically. "Two stiffs inside of two weeks is a bit too much to handle—even for a professional murder magnet like me." I pointed to the corpse lying supine across my coffee mug. "I realize it's early in the Flynn investigation, but any clue regarding the cause of death yet?"

Snip nodded. "Nothing official until we do a tox screen, stomach contents assessment, and get her on the table. But based on the paralysis of muscles of the arms, legs, and trunk of the body, my initial diagnosis is these symptoms are indicative of botulism poisoning. I'll have something definitive in the next two days."

"I'm no doctor, but if whoever poisoned Siggie used the same pricey chocolate candy Lois apparently ate, then those candy wrappers hold the answer to identifying the killer. And if botulism poisoning was in Lois's chocolate, then whoever killed the Easter Bunny also murdered the candy buyer. If Sue Ellen is behind bars, she's not responsible for poisoning my dog or murdering Lois Flynn."

Snip arched a brow. "That's a whole lotta ifs, pal."
Nothing gets past you, Doctor Quincy.

Chapter Thirty-Three

I pushed through the crowd at the newsstand next to the mart deli and bought the last copy of the *West Coast Apparel News*. The boldface two-line headline above the fold screamed. "*Bainbridge New Roach Motel: Employees go in—Don't Come Out!*"

They say any publicity is good publicity, however, two violent deaths at the flagship location of Bainbridge Department Stores aren't exactly good for the retailer's business.

I distributed their coffees to the Yentas and laid the newspaper in the center of the table.

Sonia pointed a teaspoon at the headline and clucked her tongue. "I pity *their* corporate recruiter."

I shared the details of the latest Bainbridge employee taking an unexpected dirt nap and Joan toasted me with a raised coffee cup. "And of course, our personal Murder Magnet of the Mart *naturally* discovered the second stiff."

I grinned. "What can I say? It's a gift."

Queenie leaned back in her chair and tapped an index finger on the tip of her nose. "I don't see how your theory the same person is responsible for both murders and poisoning Sigmund is possible. Let's say Michael Chennault poisoned the Easter Bunny and tried to poison Siggie." She held out her hands. "And his motive to knock off the candy buyer is…?"

I shrugged. "Maybe she supplied the jelly beans and the chocolate to him. Say he worried if the cops interviewed Lois to ask if an individual or a company bought a large amount of jelly beans and that particular chocolate brand, and she'd give the police his name. So, he eliminated her before she spilled the beans."

Hope widened her eyes. "You think he got the candy from *Lois Flynn*? How would he know her?"

Joan tsked. "He calls the Bainbridge switchboard and asks the name of the candy buyer. For all the operator knows, Michael is a candy vendor trying to make an appointment to present his line."

I tapped a spoon on the edge of the table and drummed a rat-a-tat beat. "I like him for all of it, but don't forget…Michael isn't the only one who has an industrial-sized grudge against Sue Ellen."

Queenie's back stiffened. "Don't go there, Hol." She pursed her lips. "You're barking up the wrong tree."

I held out my hand like a traffic cop at Times Square during rush hour. "Not so fast. Dixie and Lois are Bainbridge employees who both have a huge grudge against Sue Ellen. Dixie and Lois are pickleball partners on the store team. They get to know one another, spend time together—on and off the court, and discover each has been done wrong by Sue Ellen. They feed off of one another's anger and decide to make Sue Ellen pay. Since Sue Ellen's event uses jelly beans, she and Lois have to work together. Dixie and Lois do some research and find out it's easy to buy Botox online without a prescription. Dixie is on the swimwear floor during the Easter event and can plant the coated jelly beans for the Easter bunny to eat. Both women are familiar with the security camera loop and can time it so the camera doesn't pick them up doing the deed. They frame Sue Ellen for the Easter bunny's murder, and it's a win-win. They pay her back for past transgressions. Lois gets Sue Ellen's job, and Dixie doesn't have Sue Ellen interfering in hers."

Queenie wrinkled her nose. "And Siggie?"

Okay, she had me there. "Michael is most likely responsible." Or, on second thought, maybe not. I snapped my fingers. "Say the three worked together on this? Maybe Michael contacted Lois regarding the jelly beans and chocolate. Say Lois comments on how much candy Michael is buying and she asks why. Maybe he jokingly tells her and she says she wouldn't mind doing the deed herself—in fact, she has a colleague who hates Sue Ellen too...They do the deed and then Michael eliminates Lois." I waved a teaspoon at Queenie. "And if I'm right? Your pal Dixie is the next victim on Michael's hit list."

Queenie smacked her forehead. "Good grief! Are you listening to yourself? Be careful what you say before you ruin somebody's life. Words can kill the same as a bullet."

I leaned forward in my chair and growled. "Oh yeah? News flash: Don't you dare poo-poo the words just because one of the suspects is your friend. Sue Ellen may be a first-class pain in the ass, but she's *our* pain in the ass. I'm not going to let her spend the rest of her life in jail for something she didn't do."

Sonia rubbed her chin. "We're forgetting someone pretty obvious...Abby."

I dismissed her with a wave. "Abby was frustrated when she didn't get promoted, yet she said she loved working for Sue Ellen and how much she'd learned from her."

Joan pursed her lips into a funnel. "You been up to Sue Ellen's office lately? For someone *who loved* working for Sue Ellen, Abby *wasted no time* in moving herself into Sue Ellen's office."

I nodded. "I was in the office a couple of days ago and asked Abby about it. She said her desk wasn't big enough to spread out the computer reports and still write up all the orders, so she moved into Sue Ellen's. Abby said she is sure her boss will be exonerated. Once Sue Ellen returns, Abby said she'd gladly move back to her own desk."

I finished relating the latest episode of the soap opera known as my life and waited for the snappy comments from the peanut gallery to start. My clever crew of kibitzers did not disappoint me.

Joan grinned, "At the rate you call them, you're gonna get a frequent flyer card from the LA County Sheriff's office."

Sonia shook her head. "I bet they start charging you for every call."

Hope twitched her nose. "For a person who's supposed to be afraid of death, you're trying awful hard to get dead."

Queenie narrowed her eyes. "So, if you didn't accept Miguel's offer, where'd you and Siggie spend the night?"

"Siggie stayed at Muriel's and I bunked at Snip's."

She sniffed. "Whatssamatta? The service not good enough anymore at the Hotel Levine?"

I rolled my eyes. "For crying out loud, it was the middle of the night—and believe me, incurring your wrath by waking you before dawn *two times* in a week is *not* an item on my bucket list." I winced as I reached for my coffee cup. "Who knows when I might need to check in again? I didn't want to overstay my welcome by making another guest request so soon."

Eagle-eyed Joan rubbed her arms. "Those scrapes are mighty nasty."

I traced a figure eight between two of the scratches. "They're not as bad as they look. Muriel patched me up after Mark pulled me out of the water. And Snip completed the job later on." I grinned. "I bet she prefers her patients to me. They don't complain if she's not gentle during an examination."

Joan twisted her lips into a wry smile. "If you're not a helluva lot more careful, you *will become* one of her patients."

I laughed. "Funny. Snip says the same thing. As long as I was already at Snip's, I asked a few questions about Lois Flynn. Snip's not ready to call it until she does a complete autopsy. But based on the level of the paralysis of muscles of the arms, legs, and trunk of the body, her initial diagnosis is botulism poisoning…"

I held up my index finger as a wait-a-minute sign when my cell phone pinged to announce an incoming text. I read it and gave the Yentas a summation. "The text is from the sheriff's detective. *The fingerprint tests came back from the crime lab. We found six clear, full sets of fingerprints on the rail guard fitting screws. Fingerprints had a ridge density of 12 ridges/25 mm3. Based on those markers, they've been identified as female.* They eliminated my fingerprints from the sampling. Unfortunately, they got no hits when they ran the other prints through a state-wide database. They've eliminated half the world's population, including

Michael Chennault, as suspects, so the bad news is we're back to square one regarding whodunit. The good news is they've cleared my boat, so I'll sleep in my bed tonight."

I glanced at Queenie. "We owe Dixie a set of trend samples due today, right?"

Queenie nodded.

I held up the text message and Queenie squirmed in her seat.

"Then let's make the delivery in person."

Chapter Thirty-Four

We crossed onto Ninth Street after our twenty-minute meeting with Dixie and Queenie pinched her lips together as if she'd swallowed a lemon slice. "Boy, is Dixie taking Lois's death hard. Overnight, she's aged twenty years."

I held open the door at the main entrance to the mart and waved Queenie in. "No kidding. Not to be mean…Dixie didn't look much better than Lois when I discovered her body." I cast my eyes sideways. "So, whaddaya make of her reaction to my boat being vandalized?"

Queenie pressed the lobby elevator up button. "From the drop of her jaw when you told her, I'd say, genuinely shocked."

I arched a brow. "Or, she's one helluva an actress—and there's only one way to find out."

The elevator doors opened and we stepped in.

"How?"

"An innocent person volunteers their fingerprints to the cops for comparison because *they've got nothing to lose.*"

As the words came out of my mouth, my synapses snapped like a live wire and, in a moment of clarity… Good gravy. I've been wrong all along. The gears in my brain whirred. And suddenly, it all fell into place and everything became crystal clear. How could I be so blind? The whole enchilada was right in front of me all the time.

Queenie's eyes bugged as I slid my foot between the elevator doors to prevent them from closing and jumped out of the car.

I funneled my hands like a megaphone and shouted just before the doors clanged shut. "I have to check something out. If I'm right, I know who the killer is and how to prove it."

The Ninth Street traffic light turned red as I stepped into the intersection and I jaywalked to make up some time. Then fingers of doubt held me back. I might be wrong. It's happened before. Who am I kidding? I'm wrong *most* of the time.

I forced myself not to run. For once in my life, I slowed down to think through my suspicions before I jumped the gun and got myself dead. What is it that Queenie always asks? *Who has the most to lose?* Normally her reasoning is right on the money. Not this time.

Mental head slap. A klieg light couldn't blink it any brighter. How I managed to miss it, only the Goddess knows. It's not who has the most to *lose*…it's *who has the most to gain*.

Who benefitted most from a promotion?

Who benefitted most if Sue Ellen got demoted?

Who benefitted most if Sue Ellen lost her job?

Who benefitted most when Sue Ellen became the primary suspect in the Easter Bunny's murder?

Who benefitted most when Sue Ellen got arrested?

Who benefitted most from poisoning Siggie?

Who benefitted most from vandalizing my

houseboat?

Who benefitted most by stopping my investigation?

Who benefitted most by eliminating the competition for replacing Sue Ellen Magee?

No matter which path I traveled down, all roads led to only one person.

And if I'm right, Dixie Chandler is next in line for elimination.

Holy guacamole.

Hey, I can be just as myopic as a stubborn mule, but I'm smart enough to realize one thing is for sure: I've taken this investigation as far as possible on my own. Now I needed help finishing the job from someone who wears a badge and carries a gun.

I dialed Glory Washington's office number, and the call went directly to voicemail. I left a message and called Gator Goodwin next, and got the same zip-o-de-do-dah result for my trouble. Ditto for Miguel.

For someone with a precinct full of law enforcement contacts, I was running out of names. This last one was at best a long shot, but the clock was ticking. I dialed LAPD homicide detective AJ Yakamura's cell phone and crossed my fingers that she'd pick up. AJ is married to Buster Schumansky, my LA sales rep during my stint as the Ditzy Swimwear VP of sales. We stayed friends after I moved on from Ditzy to Mermaid. AJ also works for Miguel Martinez.

The detectives under Miguel's command were a tight-knit group. While she wasn't involved in the case, I had no doubt AJ had heard an earful by now from Miguel, Glory, and Gator about my interference antics. So, it came as no surprise AJ didn't answer my calls to her cell and office phone. The odds they were all out of the office at the same time were slimsky to nonesky. The more likely scenario? I'd pissed them all off big time, and they're not taking my calls. Fanfreakingtastic. I've got a killer to catch and most of the Rampart Station cops are too angry at me to respond to my calls.

Out of desperation, I dialed Snip at the office as well as on her cell. Like all the others, my calls to her also went to voicemail. I left a message asking her to get Abby's, Lois's, and Dixie's fingerprints from the Bainbridge Human Resources manager and have the crime lab run them through the system. I also asked her to pass along my messages to the cops, which even to my ears, bordered on hysterical. I prayed she listened to her voicemail a lot more often than I do mine. Who knows when or *if* one of them will return my call?

What to do, what to do? I raked my fingers through my hair. The smart money says to make a U-turn, go back to the mart, do my job, and let the cops do theirs. Fat chance of that happening. Let's face it, no one has ever confused me with Albert Einstein. Besides, I couldn't live with myself if anything happened to Dixie while I sat around with my thumb up my ass waiting for the cavalry to arrive. I squared my shoulders and headed for Bainbridge.

****

Before the doors to the executive floor elevator creaked completely open, I squeezed my tush through the narrow space and raced to the fashion offices, praying I wasn't too late. I careened around the corner and skidded into Dixie's lit open office at the end of the hall.

Her computer blinked open to a file of a half-completed spreadsheet. A copier next to the computer spat out a series of documents into a basket. Merchandised samples hung on a grid diagonally across from a wall map pinpointing all the cities Bainbridge had stores in.

Dixie's purse lay on her desk, but she was no place to be found. A person in a hurry might leave every electronic device on, but no woman walks out leaving her purse on her desk and the door wide open. Had my fears come to fruition? Had Queenie's friend become Abby's latest victim?

Mental head slap. Schlivnik, for crying out loud, get a grip. Dial it down a notch or two and don't jump to any conclusions that might embarrass the hell out of you later on. Maybe Mother Nature called and wouldn't take no for an answer. Or Dixie's demanding boss called her into a last-minute meeting. Before you look like a hysterical crazy woman to everyone on the planet, check it out.

So, for once in my life, I listened to my better angels.

I stood at the threshold of the ladies' restroom door across from the executive elevator. I cupped my hands around my mouth and shouted, "Dixie, are you in there?" Not so much as a toilet flushed. Nonetheless, I stepped into the restroom and looked under every stall door just to make sure she wasn't hiding from Abby. And for my efforts? All for nil.

I went back to the executive office section. I didn't know Dixie's boss's name. Fortunately, every office displayed a plaque next to the door announcing the name and title of the occupant. I knocked a few times on Mary Murphy's door and got no response. Maybe she was on the phone and didn't hear me? The second time, I banged my fist against the door with enough force to loosen the hinges. Still, nothing doing. I twisted the door handle, but it was locked tighter than my stingy Great Aunt Doe's purse strings. Crap.

The two most logical places?

Nothing but crickets.

Sigh.

Where the Sam Hill was Dixie?

Field trip to the mart?

Pickleball practice?

Abducted by aliens?

The answer?

My heart sank to my toes.

Only one place left.

I raced down the hall and prayed I was wrong.

Chapter Thirty-Five

The good news? The outer door to Sue Ellen's office was open. The bad news? It was the only one open on the entire aisle. If I needed any help, good luck, Schlivnik…

I was on my own.

I tiptoed into the outer office. I glanced at Abby's desk and my eyes popped. In addition to some of her cool artwork, the front page of *Beverly Hills Today*, a throwaway local paper, featured a color photo of *Dr. Max Blane* at the helm of a forty-five-foot sailboat. Was the self-described *"Dermatologist to the stars"* also Abby Blane's Botox supplier?

The door to Sue Ellen's office was three-quarters of the way open. I heard her voice, so, Abby was either on the phone or somebody was in the office. I stood between the office door and six heavy-gauge plastic bags filled to the brim with jelly beans stacked in two piles of three each on the floor next to Abby's desk.

I craned my neck and turned my head sideways to hear who Abby was talking to. Dixie Chandler? If they were talking, it's a good thing, right? Nobody died…at least not yet. I tapped the record button on my cell phone so as not to miss a single word. Abby's tone sounded conversational, and her words? Anything but. "A deal is a deal. I lived up to my part, you didn't live up to yours.

And now you're gonna die."

I angled my body perpendicular to the wall next to Abby's desk to see but not be seen. I shoved a fist in my mouth to stifle a scream. Abby aimed the gun she held steadily in her two hands directly at the head of the last person on the planet I ever expected to see.

Michael Chennault's evil laughter cackled with a curious mixture of amusement and amazement. "Oh, that's rich! *You* manage to *kill the wrong person* and still have the gall to say *I* didn't live up to my end of the deal?"

"You can't blame *me* for that. *I* didn't kill the wrong person. Sue Ellen did. I set it up perfectly. The big canister on her desk had enough poisonous jelly beans to kill an elephant." Abby huffed with righteous indignation. "It's not my fault the damned Easter Bunny ate half the jelly beans in the ginger jar and Sue Ellen took it upon herself to replenish them with the ones I put in her canister."

Abby's wicked smile was as terrifying as the devil incarnate. "The way it ended up is a win-win. Sue Ellen might not be dead, but she's still gonna spend the rest of her life in prison. The extra bonus is the freakin' Easter Bunny won't cause any more trouble. Too bad you didn't pay me everything you agreed to. Your big mistake was underestimating me. You thought you could get away paying me a pittance, stiffing me for the rest, and still expecting me to perform all the tasks as we planned." Abby waved the gun as though leading an orchestra. "Instead, you're the big loser, Mr. Big Shot. Ditzy will *never* get back into the store now and you're gonna be dead."

If I had a brain, I'd run for my life. Instead, I stood

rooted to the spot, intent on listening to these two maniacs pointing fingers at one another for the screwups of their crimes.

Michael held out his hands. "Don't be a fool. You're in the catbird seat right now. The cops are convinced Sue Ellen killed the Easter Bunny and you're gonna get her job. Don't screw things up by killing me." A shudder of fear raced down my spine as he said, "Take it from someone who knows—the cops start nosing around you when too many bodies start piling up."

How many is too many? And how does he know?

Michael took a huge wad of hundred dollar bills out of his pants pocket and threw it on the desk. "If it's only money your knickers are in knots over, take it all." Michael's tone spewed arrogance as he huffed, "Plenty more where that came from." Abby cocked the gun and Michael's voice cracked. "For God's sake, Abby! Please. I have a wife and young kids. Please don't do this. We can work it all out."

Abby's response? She sighted the gun and aimed for the spot right between Michael's eyes. Good gravy! Abby squared her shoulders and positioned herself to murder Michael in cold blood.

Why is a cop never around when you need one? What do they say? Ask and ye shall receive? The question was answered when my cell phone rang. BRRRRNG, BRRRRNG! Loudly. Mental head slap. Now's a good time to remember the vibrate function. Oops. My bad.

Abby and Michael automatically patted their pockets. While those two clowns were busy figuring out which one of their phones rang, I made a run for it. As I backed away, the heel of my shoe caught on the edge of one of the jelly bean bags. I tripped and fell unceremoniously on my ass into the left stack of jelly bean bags.

Abby pivoted sideways at the clash of concrete and flesh. The sight of me sprawled out on the floor amid an ocean of loose jelly beans sent her into hysterics. "If it isn't little Miss Persistent." My blood ran cold as she mused, "You had a helluva good run, but your luck finally ran out."

Abby pushed Michael out of Sue Ellen's office by shoving the barrel of the gun into the small of his back. "Get out there so I can see you. And don't pull any funny stuff or I'll shoot your kneecaps off just for fun before I finish you off."

Yikes.

Abby shut the outer office door with a swift kick. She smacked the cell phone out of my hand with her palm when it rang again. It hit the ground and she kicked it soccer-style into the wall and it broke into a bazillion pieces. Crap. Does the warranty cover this?

Abby waved the gun in Michael's direction. "Get next to the captain of the industry over there and let's get this thing done. "

I glared at imbecile Michael. Why didn't he rush her when he had the chance? Didn't he get the bulletin? God helps those who help themselves. Michael might be ready to die. I certainly wasn't. I slid my eyes to the right. The second stack of jelly bean bags sat tantalizingly close but just out of reach. I edged step by tiny step closer to the stack of jelly bean bags. Abby didn't shoot me. So far, so good.

I had no time to develop an actual game plan, so I punted. Words bypassed my brain and jumped out of my mouth all on their own. My heart pounded like a pile driver yet my voice rang amazingly calm. "Abby, please, you're better than this. Tell the cops you were so jealous of Sue Ellen that you were out of your mind and had no control over yourself. You might not avoid prison, but at least a sharp lawyer will get you the help you need." I flicked a wrist at Michael. "If you kill both of us, your goose is cooked. The cops aren't totally brain-dead. They'll figure it out. And I promise you, then all bets *will be* off. Don't make it worse for yourself. You're a smart woman. Abby, I'm talking to you as a friend. Please don't do this."

Any chance of talking my way out of this catastrophe slipped away as Abby dismissed me with a sweep of the gun. "My life is ruined and both of you are gonna pay." Her eyes were hard as granite as they bore into mine. "Your meddling got your dog poisoned. Your interference got Lois Flynn killed. If you didn't keep sticking your nose where it didn't belong, you wouldn't be involved in all this. But no, you couldn't let it go. I warned you over and over, yet you paid my warnings no attention." She lectured, "You should have listened, you should have taken the hint. You didn't, and this is where it brought you to." She jerked her head at Michael and spat. "Now you're another loose end I have to tie up along with *him.*"

The metallic taste of fear bit my tongue and the words she meant to comfort terrified me more. "Don't worry," she soothed. "It'll be fast. You won't suffer. My Granddaddy Asa was a hunter. I've been around guns all my life. I'm a crack shot. You'll hardly feel a thing."

Abby aimed the gun at the remainder of the stack of jelly bean bags I'd fallen into and shot a hole through the center of the last bag. Hundreds more loose jelly beans rolled all over the office floor. She giggled at her handiwork. "Now *that's* the way you roll a jelly bean."

Abby pointed the gun back at us and selfishly, I hoped this was one time ladies didn't go first. As Abby cocked the hammer, an overhead fluorescent light fixture flickered on and off. Abby instinctively turned toward the light. The time was now or never. I grabbed the two top bags of jelly beans off the other stack and slammed them into Abby's midsection with everything I had. The heavy bags made a satisfyingly loud whoomph as they hit her in the breadbasket. All the air whooshed out of her lungs and she deflated like a leaky balloon. The momentum of the hit sent her pinwheeling into the remaining stacks of jelly bean bags. Abby fired off a wild shot before she hit the ground and Michael screamed like a little girl. Abby went down with all the grace of a sack of potatoes. The irony was not lost on me. She lay buried beneath a mountain of jelly beans.

Abby dropped the gun as she fell. Remarkably, it didn't go off when it hit the ground and bounced in front of Michael. I dove for the gun but missed it. Michael had the angle and snatched it before I had a chance to grab it. He smacked the gun barrel across my mouth. Blood gushed from my lower lip and a galaxy of stars danced in front of my eyes as thunderbolts of pain stabbed my lower jawbone. I tested my jaws with a zig-zag move and three loose lower front teeth shifted.

Michael waved the gun in Abby's direction. "Get over by her."

The realization I was going to die took my breath away. If I didn't get a hold of myself, I'd never make it out of this mess alive. My loosened teeth shifted again and some of the words came out mushy. "Michael, shstop before you do someshing you can't undo."

He snickered, "It's a little late. That train already left the station." He pointed the gun at Abby. "She was gonna kill me. This is self-defense."

Blood squirted out of my split lower lip when I spoke and ran down the front of my shirt. "Why kill her? She's the murderer, not you. Hold the gun on her. Let me go for help. The cops arrive, they arresht her, and she goes to prison for the resht of her life."

"Shut up and get next to her."

Cripes, I couldn't catch a break.

Michael waved the gun under my nose. "I warned you to stay out of my business. Now you're gonna be sorry you didn't follow my instructions."

Okay, I'm a touch nosy, and now you're gonna shoot me? Seriously?

As though he read my mind, he said, "I have no choice. You know too much."

I promise to keep my yip shut.

He mused to himself, "I should have taken care of you the minute you started sticking your nose into my life." He smirked, "Who says there are no second chances? It might have been a problem explaining things to the cops before." He grinned." Now it's all gonna work out fine and dandy, thanks to you."

I took a mental bow. I live to serve.

He smiled wickedly. "When the cops arrive, I'll tell them Abby and I were working out our disagreements to get Ditzy reinstated as a Bainbridge vendor and all of a sudden, she pulled out a gun. She was furious you arrived uninvited and disrupted her plans for me. She was so pissed she threatened to shoot you first. I'm a good guy and tried to save you. I rushed her. We fought. She aimed for my head so I batted the gun barrel away. During the struggle, the gun went off. Regrettably, the gun pointed at you and she shot you dead. We wrestled. She shot me in the arm. I still managed to wrench the gun away from her. She was crazed, a maniac. She grabbed for the gun and I shot her in self-defense."

I hated the outcome, yet the story was a completely plausible one. Cripes.

"Okay, enough talk." He swept the gun to Abby. "Let's get this shindig on the road."

Just as I took a step toward Abby to appease Michael, a volcano of loose jelly beans erupted and scattered all over the office as she sat up. "That's a fabulous alibi." She gave him a round of applause and snorted her ridicule. "You'd probably get away with it. Too bad you don't have the guts to do it."

Michael grinned as wide as a Jack O'Lantern. "Gee, Abs, too bad…you're dead wrong." He dried his bloody hand on his pants, aimed the gun barrel at Abby's head, and fired a single shot. Abby's skull exploded as the bullet shattered the center of her forehead. As her body fell back and bounced around on the bed of jelly beans, her lips formed forever frozen in the shape of a surprised O.

No kidding. That makes two of us. Michael's maniacal laugh chilled my blood to ice. He sighted the gun at the same spot on my forehead. Could I possibly take him? I estimated my chances. As if. Even though he had a wounded arm, the chances of me taking a guy so much taller and stronger? Slimsky to nonesky. The element of surprise is all I had.

I swiveled my head in search of anything usable to

stop him. An array of Abby's artwork sat displayed on her desk. For once, being a shorty worked in my favor. I already stood low to the ground. Before Michael reacted, I dove to the floor. He lunged for me, but lost his balance and tripped on the loose jelly beans. I tucked my knees into my abdomen and rolled over the carpet of jelly beans like a beachball to Abby's desk. I grabbed the freeform piece of art made out of a lead pipe. I powered with my knees, wound up like a baseball pitcher, and whacked Michael squarely in his nuts.

Michael screeched as loud as a banshee and dropped hard as a rock. He rolled around on the floor holding his privates and lost his grip on the gun. To make sure he stayed down, I aimed as if a game-winning field goal was at stake and landed my kick in the center of his bloody wounded arm. He screamed again and fainted into a pile of loose jelly beans.

I grabbed the pistol off the floor and wiped Michael's blood off the gun using the tail of my shirt. I held a gun only once before and hoped I didn't shoot myself instead of him. I mentally patted myself on the back. I managed to hold the gun by the grip, not by the barrel, and aimed the business end of the pistol at Michael's head. The gun weighed a ton. I needed both hands to keep it level. Think of holding a cannon steady by your fingertips.

It didn't take long before my sweaty hands started to ache and my fingers cramped as tight as an arthritic old lady's. My leaden arms grew more numb by the minute. Soon they'd be limp as overcooked noodles. Michael was down, but he wouldn't be much longer. Help better arrive before my arms gave out at the same time as my bravado.

Why were the good guys never around when you needed them?

Finally, a male voice shouted, "Freeze!"

No problemo. I stood still as a statue.

Did somebody hear the shot and call it in?

Did the security guard finally make it up to the executive floor?

Nope. I recognized the voice.

The cavalry *finally* arrived.

Hallelujah.

I called out, "Hey, Gator. It's me, Holly Schlivnik. Detective, I'm in Sue Ellen's office. I need help. Please hurry."

Gator stopped at the open outer door to Sue Ellen's office and barked an order that was music to my ears. "Drop your weapons!"

Gladly, Detective. I set the gun on the floor and stepped on the grip. I raised my hands to the sky and cried out, "Don't shoot!" as Gator and a small army of gun-toting LAPD uniforms stormed Sue Ellen's office.

The uniforms roused Michael, cuffed him, and read his rights.

Gator cocked a brow. "*Barney Fife*? Really?"

I shrugged. "If the character fits…"

Gator grinned. "Don't make any plans on goin' into politics, ma'am."

I burst out laughing.

Then I fainted.

Chapter Thirty-Six

Two Days Later

I gently eased my pummeled bag of bones into the seat at the Yenta table and gladly let Hope serve the coffee.

Joan quipped. "Tortoises move faster, kiddo."

"Talk to me after a tortoise tangles with Abby and Michael and let's compare notes."

Queenie traced two fingers across her lips. "If you're going for the Rocky Balboa battered face look, you succeeded beyond your wildest dreams. Honestly, it's a good look for you. The split lip and the awesome shiner work nicely together. Adds character to your kisser."

At the risk of re-splitting my lip with a response matching her snark, I settled for giving her the middle finger salute.

Hope giggled. "For a nice Jewish girl, you must have the luck of the Irish watching over you." Her face clouded over. "There's no other plausible explanation for your not being dead by now."

Gee, I appreciate the vote of confidence, Hope.

Sonia spread the latest edition of the *West Coast Apparel News* out across the table and the Yentas raised their coffee cups high in a congratulatory toast.

I cringed at the boldface headline an inch above the

fold:

M X 3 MAKES MINCEMEAT OF LAPD AGAIN!

I rattled the front page of the newspaper and groaned. "Fanfreakingtastic. I'm already deep in hot water with the LAPD. This ought to put the last nail in the coffin of our relationship."

I used a teaspoon to jab at the word *mincemeat.* "And the hell of it is, my relationship with them is gonna go down the tubes over a statement that's not even accurate."

Joan clucked her disdain. "Bull puckey."

Sonia pointed a teaspoon across the table. "I'm gonna have to take Joan's side on this one, pal. The cops arrested the *wrong person.* Then they added insult to injury by blowing off your alternate suspect and never considered the possibility you had it right."

I held out my hands in supplication. "To be fair, I was just as focused as them on one suspect—who, need I remind you, also turned out to be the wrong one." I smiled sardonically. "We both got everything wrong because we muffed identifying the stakes: It was not who had the *most to lose*…it was who had the *most to gain.*"

I detailed all the points I'd figured out and tapped a spoon on the rim of my coffee cup to punctuate each one. "It didn't matter which one you chose to go down. All roads led to only one person." I surveyed the table. "If I'd asked those questions at the beginning of my investigation, Sue Ellen would have been exonerated a helluva lot sooner. Abby would be spending the rest of her life behind bars instead of taking a dirt nap. Lois would be alive…but still stuck as the candy buyer. Michael would have gone to prison too, only as an *accessory* to murder, not on a murder one charge." I hung my head. "One life almost ruined, one now spends the rest of his days in prison, and three lives extinguished…all because *I* failed to ask the right questions."

Joan glared at me over the rims of her eyeglasses. "So, Gilda Guilty, exactly who freakin' died and left you in charge?"

Sonia rubbed her chin. "It's not an issue of asking the right questions. It's more like being in the right church and sitting in the wrong pew."

I nodded my agreement. "In retrospect, you're right. All the clues were right in front of me the whole time. I just didn't put them together correctly. Abby rowed early every morning in the marina. No one pays much attention to a rower going up and down my basin. Since Michael made the veiled threat against Siggie, I assumed he poisoned my dog. Michael was on his boat the day of the incident and I assumed he monkeyed with my boat. Regrettably, I could not have been more wrong. Turns out, Abby's dad is a sailor and she grew up on boats. Abby was responsible for both." I grinned. "As usual, my wise nana got it right…whenever you *assume*, you are the first three letters of the word."

I rubbed my fingers across my face. "Abby's father is a dermatologist in Beverly Hills—he's known as the Botox Doc to the stars. When the cops interviewed Abby's father, they discovered she had pilfered small amounts of Botox from her dad's office for years. She stole the Botox to host parties to finance graduate school. She couldn't steal enough to *grow* the parties to buy a new car or turn the party profits to buy Botox online. Abby and Michael ran into each other at the marina and became friendly. Michael had a rather large side business as a drug dealer. Botox was his number one volume drug. Abby told him about her Botox parties and her problems getting the Botox. Michael started selling it to her at an unbelievably low price.

Abby said she loved working for Sue Ellen. The reality is she was furious Sue Ellen refused to promote her. After Sue Ellen threw Ditzy out of the store, Abby and Michael fed off of each other's anger and cooked up the plot to kill her.

Once Sue Ellen got arrested for killing the Easter Bunny and Abby took over the swimwear department, Michael proposed the bribe deal to get Ditzy back in the store. The scheme was to make Ditzy the predominant line in the department by slowly reducing the orders of all the other vendors over time and funneling all their volume to Ditzy. Michael envisioned a Ditzy store inside Bainbridge. While she could never have convinced her management to approve such a crazy concept, Abby was desperate for the money and did nothing to discourage his unrealistic plans.

Abby got the sniff through the office grapevine that Lois Flynn had met with the Human Resources director to discuss her getting Sue Ellen's job. When Lois got a second interview, Abby panicked. Abby couldn't take the chance Lois might prevail, so she killed the candy buyer to prevent her from getting the job Abby swore was hers."

Queenie asked, "So if Abby and Michael were tight as ticks, how'd it all go off the rails?"

"As my wise nana always said, nothing turns out the way you think it will. Michael blamed Abby for *killing the wrong person* and stopped paying her the blood money they'd agreed to. So, Abby lured Michael into

Sue Ellen's office on the pretext of working out the reinstatement details of Ditzy Swimwear to the Bainbridge supplier matrix. Once he arrived, Abby pulled a gun on him." I grinned. "Then I showed up as an extra loose end. I threw a monkey wrench into her plans and her entire scheme went to hell in a handbasket."

Hope wrung her hands. "Abby's big mistake was making a deal with the devil and believing he'd actually live up to his end of the bargain. Underestimating the power of Michael's blind ambition cost Abby Blane her life."

****

Later in the week Queenie and I sat across from one another at our partner desks in David's old office when a knock on the door interrupted our review of the monthly production schedule.

I yelled, "Come in, it's open."

David Workman studied the office he once occupied as though memorizing it as he made his way across the large room. He rested a carton containing his personal belongings on the corner of my desk and smiled sardonically. "I couldn't leave and not say goodbye."

"David," Queenie's voice caught. "Please don't do this."

I pursed my lips. "I don't get it. You said we'd given you the perfect job—no, *the job of your dreams*— expanding your creative abilities as the head merchandiser with no corporate financial responsibilities. So, if it was the job of your dreams, why are you leaving it?"

Queenie said, "We need you."

David smiled the saddest smile I'd ever seen. "No,

you don't…and that's precisely why it's time for me to move on. You *created* a position for me where there was none. Thank you kindly, but I don't need your charity." He turned to me. "Your nana used to say when one door closes another one opens, right?"

Queenie's tone was a mixture of exacerbation and angst. "This door didn't close!"

David smiled indulgently. "Yeah, Queenie, it did."

Queenie pointed a je' accuse finger at him. "Only because you've closed it!"

David chose not to respond and instead pointed to our assistant, Harriet Cowan's office adjacent to ours. "I'm leaving you in capable hands." He grinned elfishly. "If Harriet Cowan bosses you around the same way as she did me all these years, you're certain to stay on course."

He wiggled his brows. "Think you're gonna be rid of me completely? Not a chance. I passed the state real estate agent's exam and will be getting my license any day now. We're moving to Palm Springs and I'll be working as an associate at Sunset Palms Realty in charge of their new apparel industry client division." He turned the pages of an imaginary rolodex in the air. "I've got so many garment business contacts, I'll be busy morning, noon, and night." He grinned devilishly. "And since you three will be raking in the moolah hand over fist, I'll be pestering you non-stop to sell you second homes in the desert."

David hugged us both fiercely, picked up his carton, and opened the door. He turned to face us a last time and our eyes locked. I smiled as he aimed his right foot toward the doorjamb. "Bet you'd never guess I paid any attention to all your nana's traditions…better guess again…and I'm not taking any chances." He winked and stepped right foot first over the threshold. "Right foot first for me all the way." The door closed behind him and in the blink of an eye, David was gone.

David Workman gave me the opportunity of a lifetime to rise from a small company manager to an industry major league player—and for that, I'll always be grateful. But David is a man who often suffered from convenient amnesia, rarely took ownership of his actions or words, and adopted intimidation via screaming first and asking questions second as his preferred management style. He was a challenging, unappreciative boss who rather than give recognition to his employee's accomplishments, often took credit for them.

Candidly, he was one boss I often wished gone. Now that my wish had become a reality, I squirmed uncomfortably in my seat. The words of my oh-so-wise nana reverberated inside my head. "Be careful what you wish for because you just might get it."

The door closed behind him and something imperceptive shifted inside the office. One thing was certain. Our lives would never be the same.

Chapter Thirty-Seven

One Week Later

Her Supreme Royal Highness, the undisputed Queen of Swimland wasted no time getting back into the swing of things and summoned me to the inner sanctum. She gave us little more time than it took to say three Mississippi's to design and produce a capsule collection of missy and junior swimsuits and cover-up samples for a store-wide summer extravaganza to celebrate the three summer holidays: Memorial Day, the 4th of July, and Labor Day. Our design and production teams pulled out all the stops and miraculously made it happen. Now for the fun part—presenting the collection to the prickly bikini picker and hoping for the best.

I hadn't been back to Sue Ellen's office since the "*incident*" took place. The closer to my destination, the harder my heart pounded against my ribs. I arrived at her outer office door and grasped the handle. I pushed the door open, but cluck-cluck de grande me hesitated stepping across the threshold.

I craned my neck and glanced inside the room. All vestiges of the incident had disappeared as though it never happened. No yellow crime-scene tape draped the place. My nostrils were assaulted by the overpowering smell of freshly-applied paint concealing the bloodstains on the walls. No loose jelly beans covered the newly laid carpeting. Yet a shiver ran down the length of my spine as I forced myself to gingerly tiptoe inside. I fingered the surface of Abby Blane's desk and shuddered as though I'd trampled over somebody's grave. I gave myself a headshake the same way Siggie does when he's drying off from a bath and soldiered on.

I rapped my knuckles twice in a rat-a-tat-tat on Sue Ellen's closed office door. The muffled sound of two voices surprised me. Maybe Sue Ellen was interviewing Abby's replacement?

A terrifying thought twisted my heartstrings into knots. Good gravy, did I muff the meeting time? Goddess help me if I screwed this one up. Sue Ellen Magee is *not* someone who cottons to be kept waiting. I checked my watch and breathed a sigh of relief. Right on time.

Sue Ellen shouted, "Schlivnik, is that you? It's about damned time you decided to grace us with your presence. And if you have any desire to remain vertical, you'd better have my samples."

In a bit of a daze, I failed to immediately snap back a reply and she barked impatiently, "News flash, Schlivnik—contrary to popular opinion, I don't possess X-ray vision. So, get your ass in here, and lemme see the samples before we miss the damned delivery date."

This is an important event vendors clamor to participate in, so I swallowed my snippy retort. I pushed the sample crate into her office and stopped short in my tracks. Of all the people I ever expected to see Sue Ellen Magee giggling with like a couple of silly schoolgirls, Dixie Chandler is the last one on Earth. Dixie and I nodded our hellos and she smiled sardonically at the stunned expression I couldn't conceal.

I stood transfixed and kept my head on a swivel taking in the sight of Sue Ellen's packed-to-the-rafters office that had been transformed into a day at the beach. A male mannequin dressed in an old-fashioned lifeguard costume sat in a wooden lifeguard station chair in the corner holding his hand over his eyes as though searching the water for swimmers in trouble. A male and female pair of mannequins dressed in swimsuits donned in flippers, snorkels, and face masks stood next to the lifeguard station. In the opposite corner, a female mannequin and two child-sized mannequins all dressed in swimsuits sat in a plastic sand-filled pool. The three held colorful plastic pails and shovels while building a sandcastle.

A surfboard, boogie board, jet ski, two mesh beach chairs draped by a pair of colorful terrycloth beach towels, and an unfurled canvas beach umbrella leaned against the wall behind Sue Ellen's desk.

Sue Ellen stood in front of a large grid on wheels covered by samples organized into groups merchandised by color story. A second grid held old-fashioned one-piece swim costumes from the turn of the last century. Dixie stood next to a third grid that held an open schematic floor plan of the swimwear department furled across it.

Sue Ellen and I locked eyes as I angled my head in Dixie's direction. She cackled without a scintilla of irony in her tone. "Hey, if you can't beat 'em, then join 'em."

Then the bitch of bikinis was all business. She pointed to the sample crate. "Okay, Schlivnik, organize the samples by category and color story and lay them across my desk."

Once I complied, she and Dixie made their

selections and hung them on the grid next to the other samples.

Sue Ellen grabbed three junior bikinis that had Ditzy Swimwear hangtags attached to them off the grid and waved them under my nose. "Michael Chennault may be out of the picture, but Ditzy has not been reinstated to the Bainbridge vendor matrix." She snapped, "I don't appreciate you and Hope sneaking Ditzy samples into the styleout. If Ditzy wants back in, let whoever is now running the company schedule a pitch appointment and we'll see if we have a place for them."

I poked an index finger into my cleavage. "That would be me."

Sue Ellen sputtered like a car missing a sparkplug. "W-hat w-would b-be y-you?"

I waited a beat before answering—to revel in the delicious pleasure of her confusion.

"The person now running the company."

I took the samples out of her hands and fingered a Ditzy hangtag. "After Michael Chennault got arrested, his wife reached out to us. She is a successful Beverly Hills realtor and has no desire to run a swimwear company. She asked if we were interested in purchasing Ditzy. We said maybe… She asked us to make an offer. We ran the numbers past our accountant and he said they looked good. We made an offer and Mrs. Chennault accepted. The transfer of ownership was finalized three days later. Ditzy Swimwear is now completely integrated into the Mermaid Swimwear product matrix." I pointed to the swimwear department floor plan schematic. "We're gonna need a substantial increase in junior open to buy to support the additional floor space."

Sue Ellen huffed self-righteously. "You know

better. My business is not for sale. Vendors have to *earn* a place on my floor. So, if your game plan was to garner special treatment by proving my innocence, you should have let me rot in jail."

Now you tell me…

Scoring additional swimwear orders from Sue Ellen Magee was *definitely* the first thing that came to mind when Abby Blane aimed her gun at my head.

No good deed goes unpunished from the buyer we all love to hate.

Welcome back, Queen of Mean.

We missed you.

Thank you for purchasing
this publication of The Wild Rose Press, Inc.

For questions or more information
contact us at
info@thewildrosepress.com.

The Wild Rose Press, Inc.
www.thewildrosepress.com